# MERRY-MAKING IN OLD RUSSIA

EVGENY POPOV was born in 1946 in the Siberian city of Krasnoyarsk. Unable to gain access to either the Gorky Institute of Literature or the Institute of Cinematography, from 1963 until 1968 he studied at the Moscow Geological Institute. In 1976, he made his literary debut in the leading journal *Novy mir* with two stories, which were introduced by the popular Siberian writer Vasily Shukshin, who praised the younger writer but hinted that his literary career would not be an easy one. In 1979, with Vasily Aksyonov, Andrei Bitov, Viktor Erofeev and others, Popov edited *Metropol*, an anthology of unorthodox writing which the editors requested should be published uncensored. Permission was refused, and *Metropol* circulated first as a samizdat text, and was published in the West in 1981. For his part in the affair Popov was immediately expelled from the Writers' Union, which, like a character in one of his own stories, he had only succeeded in joining a matter of months before and from then until 1987 he was unable to publish in Russia. However, since *glasnost* and the subsequent collapse of the Soviet Union, like other writers of the "lost generation", Popov's works have been widely available. Three novels and several collections of stories have appeared, as well as a number of plays. *The Soul of a Patriot*, his first book to appear in English translation, was warmly greeted on its publication by Harvill in 1994. A vice-president of the Russian PEN Club (founded 1989), Popov is much admired for his open-mindedness, wit and good sense.

ROBERT PORTER, the translator, is Reader in Russian Studies at the University of Bristol, the author of *Four Contemporary Russian Writers* (Rasputin, Aitmatov, Vladimov and Voinovich), and the translator of *The Soul of a Patriot*. His most recent work of criticism is *Russia's Alternative Prose*.

*Other books by Evgeny Popov available in Harvill editions*

THE SOUL OF A PATRIOT

*Evgeny Popov*

# MERRY-MAKING IN OLD RUSSIA

*Translated from the Russian*
*by Robert Porter*

THE HARVILL PRESS
LONDON

All the stories in this collection are selected from *Zhdu lyubvi neverolemnoi* (Sovetskii pisatel, 1989) with the following exceptions: "The Reservoir", which first appeared in the anthology *Metropol* (Ardis, 1981), "Merry-making in Old Russia", which first appeared in the collection *Veselie Rusi* (Ardis, 1981), and "The Spiritual Effusions and Unexpected Death of Fetisov", which appeared in the journal *Volga*, No. 3, 1990. At the author's request, the *Metropol* texts of four stories ("Robber", "Cat Catovich", "Why You're Always Broke" and "Mountains") have been used rather than the very slightly adapted texts appearing in *Zhdu lyubvi neverolemnoi.*

This English translation first published 1996 by
The Harvill Press
84 Thornhill Road
London N1 1RD



This work was translated with the financial support of the European Commission



A CIP catalogue record for this title is available from the British Library.

ISBN 1 86046 197 2

Designed and typeset in Sabon at
Libanus Press, Marlborough, Wiltshire

Printed and bound by Butler and Tanner
at Selwood Printing, Burgess Hill

# CONTENTS

# Translator's Preface

Here is Evgeny Popov's Russia – a primitive settlement or a prospector's camp out in Siberia, a shabby railway station on the outskirts of Moscow, a new co-operative flat, or a peasant hut, the factory workshop, or the manager's office. His characters may be eccentrics, often in a child-like state, caught between the harsh routine of everyday existence and the occasional trappings of the modern world. In their confusion and frustration, they resort to vodka, physical and verbal abuse or – like their creator, but without his self-awareness – to metaphysical enquiry. They may tell each other stories, sometimes tall stories, and they imagine things so vividly that at times common sense and reality go by the board.

Written and set in the Soviet period, the stories in the present volume for the most part remained unpublished in the author's homeland, until the Soviet Union was on its last legs. One enthusiastic editor suggested to the author that he relocate his narratives in America and then they might stand a chance of bypassing the censor! Popov's sense of the ridiculous certainly has its roots in the real world.

The manner of this fiction can also be traced back to the genre of the fantastic, exemplified best in the nineteenth century by Nikolai Gogol. However, there are also clear echoes of the modernist and absurdist prose of the 1920s. Popov may well take his cue from Mikhail Zoshchenko's short stories, with their earthy dialogues and off-beat characters, yet his voice remains distinctly his own, a curious blend of quirky comedy and serious contemplation.

The language of Popov's fiction combines Soviet cliché with time-honoured Russian vernacular. Yet the bathos and parody thus engendered run much deeper than political satire – the author is as likely to cock a snook at the Russian classics as at the Five Year Plan. Some of the stories are a reworking or an inversion of the traditional fairy tale. Cinderella is likely to get pregnant at the ball and Prince Charming will in all probability be an alcoholic. And the happy ending? – sometimes no ending at all, just a shift in perspective which questions the validity of all that the reader has perceived so far, sometimes a promise of another story. Indeed, the stories do interlock at times. Names, faces and locations recur; the vastness and ambitious thinking of the old Soviet empire are reduced to the dimensions of the family, a group of chance acquaintances, the street corner, the price of a bottle.

Despite this, Popov's heroes have their loftier aspirations, and sometimes a sense of disquiet invades their lives, as the mundane becomes the macabre. Death is never far away. A chilly Siberian wind blows through the slapstick and the burlesque, through the workplace, the home and the seedy eating houses, a wind which touches us all.

ROBERT PORTER
Bristol, February 1996

# MERRY-MAKING IN OLD RUSSIA

# Five Tales about Vodka

*There is no point in warning you, respected reader, that the tales which you are about to read after this preface by me and then another one, come from the pen of a remarkable man, the late Nikolai Nikolaevich Fetisov and comprise a trifling little part of his huge literary legacy. This you will realize for yourself by his brilliant style, the fast pace of the action in the tales and by the exceptional topicality of the subject matter treated by the deceased. Nikolai Nikolaevich is, as it were, saying to us: "Yes! We really do still have some people who abuse the confidence shown in them. We do, but they will soon be gone."*

Evg. Popov

My dear people! Good people! I should warn you that the five tales about vodka which I present here are directed exclusively against alcoholism, are a contribution to the struggle against it. And if anyone spots anything else in these tales, then that's his own business. And it's only his own business, if he keeps what he's spotted to himself and doesn't publicize it. Because there's a lot that I will put up with, but eventually I'll sue someone for slander. And the man will find himself up in court answering good as gold to the magistrates and to me. It's high time we put a stop to people looking for symbolism in my stories and reading juicy bits between the lines. And on top of that, it's high time I was published in huge print-runs and paid good money for my work. Juicy bits are like bedbugs.

Nik. Fetisov

# *Chair Chair Stoolovich*

There was once a man, terribly fond of vodka, who on one occasion drank in the following fashion: he bought a very big bottle of vodka, got a glass and started drinking out of the bottle and the glass.

After partaking of a certain quantity this very same man felt that his life had become considerably brighter.

And he moved from the little stool which old women love to put their feet up on. He sat down on a chair of the kind that you find these days in every house and in every peasant hut. These days you find chairs and stools everywhere.

He sat down, and the man's mood went from strength to strength. And the chair became too low for him! He put the little stool on the chair, clambered up, and continued his drinking from bottle and glass.

Now, as everyone knows, the meaning of life for man resides in his never stopping at what he has achieved. Everyone knows that if a man stops at what he has achieved, then he would revert to his primitive state and would be dancing naked round a camp fire.

And that's why today we have almost no one at all dancing round camp fires. On the contrary: turbines produce an electric current and the whole country is illuminated by its magical light.

So therefore the man went into the kitchen and fetched a red-coloured three-legged chair, which had been made in the city of Riga (in The Soviet Socialist Republic of Latvia).

He placed the red chair on the ordinary chair, and on the red chair he placed the little stool, and sat right up on top, remembering quite clearly that he still had another large bottle of vodka.

From his perch, he surveyed fervently all the furniture around him, which he had earned with his own hands. The lamp standard he'd earned with his own hands. The piano for his daughter who was away at a Pioneer camp he'd earned with his own hands. The German ottoman he'd earned with his own hands. And also, unafraid of the consequences, he had sent his wife off on holiday to Sochi.

"I ought to buy a carpet as well, a reversible mat. When the missus comes back, we'll go and see Ivan Ivanych in the shop and buy it," said the man.

Alas! Alas! How often our wishes fail to keep pace with the swift flow of life as it unfolds! No sooner had the drunkard uttered these sensible words than the edifice he had constructed began to wobble and our hero, Chair Chair Stoolovich, crashed with tremendous force to the floor, implanting his head in the latter, as per the universal law relating to falling down in a drunken state.

Chair Chair Stoolovich's head suffered a great deal from the fall. He took headache pills. The headache pills didn't help. He went to the doctor, and the doctor told him that his brain had shifted as a result of the trauma.

And so the man passed away, leaving a wife and daughter to sob over his stupid body. Before his death he really let himself go to pieces, got rid of all the furniture, except the piano, and drank the proceeds.

It will be obvious to everyone that Chair Chair Stoolovich's wife and daughter will not be lost in our country of the Soviet Union . . . The daughter will finish school, and perhaps, will even become a professional pianist. And if she doesn't – that's no great tragedy. His wife will find herself another man, because she's a good-looking woman.

But this is a disgrace! You imagine how hurtful it was to them to see their dear drunkard not at the dinner table, but in a coffin.

Can you imagine where we'd be if all drunkards started falling off chairs and dying? It could be such a powerful shock to their children's tender souls, that they in turn could quite easily start drinking, and thus create a chain reaction of drunkenness.

## *O-D-Cologne*

The neat and orderly work of the turning shop at the industrial rubber goods plant was a joy to behold. The faces of the workers were serious and intense. The bearings of the steel trimmer whirled round. The white emulsion flowed merrily about. And only as soon as there was a break did you get joking and laughter. Then the dominoes started rattling and everyone told stories about what he'd seen in his life.

Petrov and Popov were the two turners who had seen more than the others in their lives. All the others found it a pleasure to listen to them, crowding around and treating them with universal regard and deference.

Not just because they had seen a lot in life but also because they regularly over-fulfilled their work norm by a large percentage.

Yet in actual fact they were two completely different characters. Popov was fat and happy-go-lucky, drank nothing but beer, and then only on state holidays.

Petrov was just the opposite. He was skinny and tall. He'd had his right kidney removed. He was a nervous type. He drank not only on state holidays, but on Sundays as well. And on Saturdays too. And more than once when he was drunk he boasted of the fact that he drank not vodka, but common or garden Troinoi eau-de-Cologne.

"What do you see in eau-de-Cologne, you idiot?" his colleagues would ask him.

"I see everything in it," Petrov would answer importantly, drinking his eau-de-Cologne instead of vodka. But I must repeat, he was a first-rate worker.

Now it came about that competition in the workshop for who could do the best work stepped up sharply.

They all worked flat out. Important initiatives were undertaken. The struggle to economize on materials was stepped up. And of course, ahead of them all, were Popov and Petrov. They worked away, egging each other on, and the work went at a cracking pace.

The time came to tot up the results. And here an extraordinary thing happened. Popov's and Petrov's indicators turned out to be exactly the same. On all scores. In output, and in economizing. When they came to establishing who should be awarded first place, they couldn't reach a conclusion.

"Maybe we could put one of them in second place?" some people suggested, wishing to settle the whole thing.

But other people who wanted to settle the whole thing objected: "How can we do that? Why does one of them have to suffer, and the other one come out on top at his expense?"

You'd find it interesting to take a look at those responsible for the argument. If this had taken place in some other, less closely knit collective, then maybe they would be grousing at each other, and possibly even having a punch-up. But not here. Calmly and deliberately they just carried on grinding the machine components, just occasionally ribbing each other with inoffensive witticisms.

For example, one day Popov announced: "Comrade Petrov stinks like that because he's got a carburettor inside him. He runs on eau-de-Cologne."

Then it dawned on them all. And one comrade promptly said to another: "I feel that we can't award the first place to comrade Petrov, because we can't award the first place to a comrade who's always guzzling eau-de-Cologne."

"And always bragging about it into the bargain," agreed the comrade who had been addressed.

These were the sort of conversations that started to do the rounds of the workshop. And when Petrov heard them, a change came over his face.

"No. O-D-Cologne has got nothing to do with it," he said in the smoke room. I've always done a fair day's work and if I drink O-D-Cologne that's my business. You drink kvass, don't you, and I don't have it in for you. I drink O-D-Cologne, so you just lay off me."

But similar black propaganda concerning the filthy drink only made him seem all the more guilty. His comrades held serious consultations and then brought matters to a head: they not only deprived Petrov of the first place, they also produced a disgusting picture of him in the wall newspaper spraying something into his mouth from a canister. Eau-de-Cologne.

But they commissioned an 10 x 8 inch photograph of Popov and hung it up in a prominent place, with a caption which spelled out Popov's good work.

That day many people saw Petrov. And his little face became all the more pinched, he kept twisting his head around like a wolf and saying quietly: "I don't understand it. This is right out of order. What have I been doing a fair day's work for? So that they can draw a picture of me looking like a tart? I don't want any of this. I never agreed to work under these conditions. It's not fair. But, have it your way, I'll hang there, if that's what you want."

At this juncture the attention of his comrades should have been directed to his somewhat strange words. After all, they had acted in a rather tactless manner. It was most certainly necessary to punish Petrov and to explain to him the harm that could be done by using eau-de-Cologne as a comestible. It was necessary to do so, but not so bluntly. It should have been done a bit more gently.

And that's what a lot of people thought the following morning when they arrived at the workshop and discovered the following terrible spectacle hanging there, before the police and the ambulance arrived.

Hanging there. He was hanging there. Petrov had hanged himself with his own trouser belt. He had hanged himself in the same prominent place where the photograph of his fellow contestant hung.

When they came close to him the doctors and policemen were astonished to detect a whiff of eau-de-Cologne about the hanged man. But then everything was explained to them, and then the doctors put the troubled minds of the workers' collective at rest by saying that Petrov, being an inveterate alcoholic, had committed suicide while in a state of alcoholic depression. And therefore the collective bore no responsibility at all for his pathologically induced actions.

## *Freedom*

A young man, wanting to see the girl he loved, was waiting for her, as they had agreed, by the musical comedy theatre, where she worked as the properties girl, though this was her day off.

The girl was late and the young man fell deep in thought. He thought hard, but just could not understand it: why didn't the girl want to go the whole way with him, despite the fact that they had already drunk vodka together several times and had been in bed naked together three times.

Would-be theatre-goers were scrounging spare tickets off of one another. A cheerful crowd rolled up in a taxi. They got out. A curly-headed chap with a bald patch said to his female companions: "Know what, girls?"

"What?" asked the girls, the youngest of whom was a hundred years old.

"Well, you know this musical comedy, let's forget it," joked the chap. "Let's go to the kebab house instead. I'll introduce you to a Georgian there. He's my best friend!"

"We'd like to meet a Georgian," declared the girls decisively and started to titivate themselves. The curly-headed chap with the bald patch traded in the tickets and the group disappeared.

"Oh, f— your mother," mumbled the young man.

"What you going on about my relatives for?" said an indignant voice, interrupting his train of thought.

And the owner of the voice appeared before him. He stood there, swaying. The young man turned away.

"Don't you turn yer mug away from me," still swaying, said the scruffily dressed man, reproachfully. "You're a layabout, and I'm a working man. I'm the joiner here, but the assistant manager just grabbed me by the lapels and said: 'Clear off, you shit. Tomorrow you can write me a letter of explanation as to why you got drunk at work.'"

The young man looked at his watch.

"She's not coming, the bitch," he mumbled. "The cow's got it coming to her now, just like I promised."

And this is what he had promised her. He'd rung her up at work and said: "I'm coming to your place tomorrow."

"No, don't come," said the properties girl, who lived in a wooden barracks house in Zasukhina Street.

"I'm coming round to your place tomorrow and if you're not home, I'm going to smash all your windows and tell the neighbours what kind of a girl you are."

"What kind of a girl am I?" asked the properties girl, livening up.

"You know yourself," replied the love-smitten young man gloomily.

After which, he was accorded a date at seven-thirty. Just before the show started.

"I've got to talk over a few things with my friends first," explained the properties girl.

And she'd deceived him and stood him up. The bitch.

"That's it. I'm going to break all her windows," said the deceived young man, furiously.

"That's right," said the drunk. "That's right. Smash things up, give her a good hiding. Who was it who robbed me last week? Nicked a half bottle off me by the shop. It's just like you lot. They give you rats, you youngsters, freedom, and you start showing off. And who's going to give me freedom? The assistant manager slung me out on my neck. And my wife's going to give me a good hiding for sure when I get home. She's crafty. Every time I get smashed she lets me have it with the rolling pin. In the morning I think that I've fallen over somewhere, so I don't beat her up for it. She deceives me."

"You don't know Dunka, the properties girl, do you?" asked the young man curiously.

"Of course I do, why shouldn't I. She works with me. I've got money, you know. Don't you go thinking I'm a dropout. I'm a working man. I've got money."

And the drunkard pulled some ridiculous bits of paper out of his crumpled pocket.

"Couldn't you just pop along there and call her for me?" asked the young man, growing angry with himself.

"I'm not going on my own," said the joiner, making bones about it. "If there's a couple of us, then I'll go. Let's go together. We can have a beer. We can get a beer in the theatre canteen."

The young man felt down-hearted. But also curious as to what the canteen was like. And if there were real live actors there. The young man held real actors in great respect. That was how he had got to know Dunka. His mates had said to him: "Have you got a woman?"

"Yes, I have," replied the young man, "she works in the theatre."

"Bet she likes a fuck then," said his mates, who had perverse ideas on many subjects.

And the young man had laughed.

They went in by the stage door. An elderly man who looked like a cockerel was sitting at a table.

"Where do you think you're going?" he said to the joiner, who was pretty unsteady on his feet.

"This young man is looking for his sister," said the joiner, with a wink to the young man.

The latter was blushing, but they were let in.

"You go and find Dunka for me, and I'll be on my way," mumbled the young man timidly.

"Inna mint, inna mint," said his escort, who by now had started speaking very bad Russian. "Inna mint. Lesh have a beer firsht."

So they got to the canteen. The canteen turned out to be the same as any other, with the exception of the clientele. The clientele was – my God! There was a cowboy sitting down playing with various revolvers. A beautiful woman was fanning herself with a great big fan. A red lamp came on above the entrance and the cowboy bounded off smartly. Somewhere from afar his voice rang out in betrayal: "I'm gonna kill you, you no-good bum! You've poisoned my life. Oh, Mary, Mary! My beautiful Mary."

The young man was telling the joiner about his love life.

"I'll smash them, I'll smash her windows, the rotten cow," he was saying.

And all the while he was treating the theatre employee to drinks.

And the latter was by now in a complete trance. In a deep, deep trance, but then he got to his feet and burst into song:

*Oh, give it me! Give me freedom!*

After which he collapsed on the floor and couldn't get up again.

The woman working in the canteen and the clientele waited with interest to see how the young man would react to his fellow-drinker's demise, because the young man himself was spick and span, neatly groomed and wearing a nice sweater.

But all he did was get a bottle of wine instead of beer and just started drinking alone.

"Just look, our joiner there wanted freedom," said one ruddy-faced actor to a pale-faced actor.

But the latter wasn't in the best of moods and replied angrily: "A man doesn't need freedom. He just says that he needs freedom for the sake of appearances. He needs illusion, not freedom. Give our joiner an illusion and he'll be happy as the day is long. But if you give him freedom – he'll destroy everything, and first of all himself."

"What's all this then, Vasily, is that the sort of philosophy they taught you at drama school?" asked the ruddy-faced actor with a laugh.

"Here's to me," said the young man loudly, raising his glass.

And while this was going on, his beloved Dunka was close by, sitting on a costume box and swinging her legs. Her female friends informed her that they had seen her fancy man in the canteen, drunk and angry. Dunka felt scared but she felt good too. She wanted more cognac and Pigeon's Milk sweets.

## *The Diver Who Was Lucky at First but then Was Done for*

A piss artist was with a small group of people celebrating International Child Protection Day. The drunkard didn't care what the exact occasion was as long as it was a public holiday.

And the group was small, but intellectual. A doctor, a visiting actor, and a couple of girls who nobody knew. The alcoholic didn't have a partner so he was a bit miserable.

And they were having an interesting conversation too, very topical. The doctor and the actor were expressing their views on the issue of technological progress interfering with the life force of nature.

"You'll forgive me, but I simply can't agree with you on that point," said the doctor, blowing smoke rings.

"No. A thousand times no," reiterated the actor. "You must forgive me, but no. It's a good thing after all. You just imagine – there was nothing there, just cliffs, and now there's a hydroelectric station there."

They drank some vodka, the alcoholic kept silent.

"Ah, my dear actor friend," said the fairly inebriated doctor. "You've only just arrived here. It's easy for you to talk. But my grandfather used to live here, my grandmother lived here, my great grandfather lived here, my great grandmother lived here. Of course, it's – I'm not arguing against having the hydroelectric station. Not at all," and he gesticulated with his hand.

"But you have to understand. It's a hydroelectric station. You can choose to build a hydroelectric station or you can choose not to build it. You could contemplate there the use of say, atomic fuel. But how are you going to rebuild the natural beauty that has disappeared? The forest? The cliffs?"

"Listen here, they've cleared all the forest anyway, cut it down."

"All of it? Have you been down to the sea? Have you seen what the coastline's like? It's pure surrealism. There are trees there. The tops are sticking up out of the water, and you dive down into their roots. Scary, diving down to their roots, isn't it? Well, actually, I'm telling lies. I've never tried it."

"No. You can dive there all right," interceded one of the girls. "It's warm there, but you can't in the Enisei. The water's four degrees all the year round there."

"Why's that?" asked the actor in astonishment.

"Because the water at the bottom flows over the reach of the dam and there isn't time for it to warm up again before it reaches the town," explained the erudite young lady.

The alcoholic kept silent. Then the other girl intervened.

"Well, you wouldn't catch me diving in the sea. In the first place you can pick up an infection there. They used to bury diseased cattle there, that's where the infection comes from. And in the second place, I used to live in that district, my daddy is buried there, and now he's under water. How can I go diving in on top of my daddy?"

The maiden let slip a tear and took a drink all in one movement. The doctor was also upset, and wishing to offer a word of comfort, spoke as follows: "Now you're mistaken there. There can't be any infection there. They've installed concrete overhangs. There can't be any infection there."

"Overhangs over all the diseased cattle?" said the maiden doubtfully.

The doctor lost his temper.

"Can't you see, you idiot, that it's got nothing to do with cattle, nothing at all. Nor even with cemeteries. We're talking about beauty! Beauty is disappearing under the onslaught of progress . . . though, anyway, the cemetery . . . yes, there is an argument there too," he muttered.

The maiden took fright at these sharp words. The actor was no longer arguing. His female friend was sitting in a relaxed pose, and he had noticed a blue vein on her leg in the shape of a letter M.

"Metro. Man," said the actor.

"What, what?" they asked repeatedly.

And the alcoholic still kept silent, silent, silent. And then ended his silence.

When they all started asking "What, what?", the alcoholic raised his unruly head and said with total irrelevance: "What's all this narrow-minded talk for, comrades? Why can't you go diving? 'Course you can go diving."

Whereupon he dashed the full length of the one-roomed, first-floor flat and dived out of the window, smashing through the double frames.

The other drunks rushed over in horror and saw the alcoholic lying in the grass, on the freshly ploughed earth.

"We've got to run down there quick and see what's happened to him," shouted the drunks, and they rushed downstairs to see what had happened to the diver.

But when they got down there, they couldn't find the diver, it was as if there were no trace of the catastrophe. People who happened to be passing by could give them no explanation. They simply shied away from the excited drunks. While the search continued, night fell imperceptibly, the man who had vanished had vanished without trace, and they went back to the flat, where they fell asleep imperceptibly.

The diver had been very lucky at first. He had fallen onto some ploughed land, and when he came to, he was overjoyed to be alive. Fearing the worst, he felt all his limbs and discovered that they were all there. But his fear didn't leave him. So the drunkard leapt to his feet, charged off to the nearest casualty department and asked for some medicine. They gave him a thorough examination and told him not to talk rubbish about falling from the first floor of a block of flats.

But, with tears in his eyes and ardour in his soul, the drunkard swore to God that it was true.

Yes! Those medical people would have found themselves in a difficult position, if one of them hadn't had the good sense to give the drunkard a breathalyzer test.

The diver blew into the tube and was done for immediately. They kept him in for a time and in due course he was transferred to Detoxification Centre No.1, where he was stripped naked and put under a cold shower.

He had a dreadful night. They kept bringing in drunks. Two of them had a fight, and the policeman gave them a stern warning. One of them was sick.

The next morning the drunk was fined thirty roubles and his employers were informed of his misbehaviour. The drunkard had to explain himself to his comrades. He stood before them and suffered agonies.

## *Romasha and Julietta*

A total piss head by the name of Romasha, whom, if that wasn't enough, all the girls were crazy about, brought one of them back to his place once, and there they started drinking vodka, one using the glass, and one drinking straight out of the bottle.

Yes! The girl was drinking too, having utterly forgotten her maidenly honour. She drank as if she didn't know how harmful vodka is to a young, undeveloped human organism. She drank as if she'd never read the newspapers, never heard the radio, never seen the television!

The poor girl! Maybe she was behaving so badly because she was in love. After all, she really did love the alcoholic Romasha very much.

And she had good reason to love him. He had been very clever until the drink finally got the better of him. He knew off by heart the dates of great people and he loved talking about the hardships they had had to suffer. She loved him.

And incidentally, Romasha loved her very much too. He had started to love her at the time when he only drank in the evenings and only moderately. And at that time she was a beautiful girl and only laughed at him when he made advances to her.

How this drove him to despair! She laughed and that made him die. Once he even put his fist through a window, and he also got the drinking habit.

He was from the outset a weak person, as you can see, but the immoderate drinking gave him a surrogate strength of character. He was cheeky, witty. Those silly girls came flocking round him and he indulged the lot of them. He started being rude to people and acting strange.

But a girl is a funny creature! As soon as she saw that her erstwhile chum was guzzling vodka like a horse and getting his leg over every bit of skirt that came his way, she promptly, immediately, instantly – fell in love with him herself.

And she started coming round to his flat. At first he didn't understand what was going on. He thought that the girl was just mocking him. But when he finally caught on, he panted with delight, and started making love to the girl breathlessly whenever they had any free time.

And free time was something that they had a lot of, because Romasha was by now reduced to working at the cemetery, drawing *in memoriam* plaques for anybody that wanted them.

And the girl, well she was a girl. She could always find free time. Generally speaking, girls always have everything, they can always get some money from God knows where, and they can always give a lad the price of a bottle.

So, they got used to each other. The silly couple should have left it there for the moment. After all, it was a very fine moment for them.

But the drunkard just couldn't forget how she had led him up the garden path before. That is, on the surface he had long since forgotten, but underneath, there inside . . . Do you know how dark it is there inside?

And the girl too, she felt ashamed in the eyes of other people and in her own eyes, because however strong she had tried to be, she had still fallen for a good-for-nothing, who had no future, no money, no authority, no powerful friends, no car.

Given this situation, the vodka flowed in rivers, while Romasha found himself writing fewer and fewer plaques. Then he wrote some poetry and read it to the girl:

*I was told by an alcoholic*
*That she was a catholic.*
*Now I know: among alcoholics*
*You find quite a lot of catholics.*

That's what he read to her. The girl looked at him inertly, went to the bathroom, and when she came back, laid into the vodka again.

"Pour me some too," asked Romasha.

The girl sighed again, looked at him again, but poured him some out.

And she came to him while he was lying in the dirty bed.

"My darling," she said. "My darling. You're mine."

"I adore you," he said. "I adore you, I adore you. You've ruined me, but I adore you. I adore you."

"I'm done for as well," answered Julietta. "I wanted to marry someone with some sort of higher degree, but I'm done for. I can't marry someone with some sort of higher degree. You're the one for me, my little one, my joy."

And they drank the vodka, and they were intimate, and when they had finished, the alcoholic lay on his back. He looked at the ceiling and thought about the history of mankind and he knew that she was lying next to him: she was one metre sixty-eight tall, her heart was pounding away, pumping seven litres of blood around, there was a blue vein on her wrist.

"My darling," whispered the girl, half asleep. "My darling. You're my little one, you're strong and brave. Shall we have some more vodka, do you fancy some?"

And then, at last, the alcoholic made up his mind. His face burned with a soft glow. He took the girl in his arms. Her full lips were moist, and her hair covered her face.

And he took the girl in his arms, went out on to their fifth-floor balcony, and looked at the city stretched out below.

And he looked intently at the city stretched out below. The girl embraced him weakly. He leant over the railings and let go of the girl. She didn't scream. There was a dull thud. A dark patch spread out over the asphalt. The alcoholic stood on the balcony.

And this whole hideous picture of plummeting morals was seen by the domino-players outside, now rooted to the spot, in the middle of their game of Matador under the shady poplar tree. They worked at the combine factory and, rooted to the spot, didn't know how to interpret what had happened. The alcoholic stood on the balcony.

"Oy, hey you!" shouted one of the domino players.

The alcoholic wasn't listening to him.

"Hang on. Don't rush. I'm just coming," he mumbled, after which he too threw himself off the balcony. On the way down all the wisdom of the world was revealed to him. But unfortunately, people who have had all the wisdom of the world revealed to them are not in a position to tell anyone about it afterwards.

They had no clothes on. The domino players covered the bodies with sheets they brought from home and waited for the representatives of the police and health services to arrive, while cursing and swearing at the ghoulish crowd of on-lookers to keep away.

* * *

Dear people! Good people! Fellow countrymen! You can see from the example of the five tales about vodka presented to you here, that people who drown themselves in a sea of vodka have a very, very tough time of it.

But it must also be hard on those who sail on the surface of this expanse of hard drink in a snow-white liner. There he stands, leaning on the stern, the son of a bitch, wearing an immaculate sodding dinner jacket and listening to the ship's orchestra playing "Farewell, Slav Girls", while the restaurant is serving red caviar.

He ought to be ashamed of himself, a man like that! He ought to be very, very, ashamed of himself for not struggling against this sea of vodka and seeing to it that it dries up once and for all. He ought to be very ashamed of himself!

But on the contrary, he's not ashamed at all. Moreover, he'll probably hold a grudge against me for writing these five tales about vodka.

But how can I help writing five tales about vodka when I can hear the howls of families falling apart and I see little children with their faces contorted with anguish.

It's hell everywhere. And there's vodka, vodka, vodka everywhere!

Fog! Disease! Gloom! I feel it will soon be autumn. In the morning I will lean out of the window and see an alcoholic walking along a railway track, silver with hoar frost, going I know not where.

# Merry-making in Old Russia

This really weird suicide story ended badly for one old man. That morning he had read in the newspaper that alcoholism in our country was now more or less on the way out, and that the solution to the whole problem was to have the stuff sold in "quarter bottles" and "halves" instead of in full litre bottles. He read this and was so touched by the sincerity of the article that it brought tears to his eyes, yet come evening, he upped and got smashed again.

This distressed his wife, old Maria Egipetovna, who got a pension of thirty-two roubles a month and took in laundry from the neighbours' lodgers – thin-lipped youngsters doing their first year as civil aviation pilots.

The pilots were all great philanderers, going to restaurants and concerts, riding around in taxis – that was why they demanded that their laundress provide them with snow-white shirts and stiff, starched collars, so that a black tie would stand out against the white and convey to all those around them a notion of the young man's youthful bravura, neatness and strength. When they collected their bundles of clean washing, the pilots would hum: "He, he encha-a-anted me, that la-a-ad, that air-bo-o-rne lad!"

Two of his drinking companions brought the old man home. They leaned him up against the door, banged hard on the window and ran off, fearing a verbal confrontation with Maria Egipetovna, and apart from that, seized by a burning desire to lay their hands on some more cash somewhere and do some more drinking, because they were young, just like the pilots in the lodgings, and were in work: one as a turner, and the other as a metal-worker and sanitary engineer, and right now they wanted to get thoroughly drunk, and be ready to fight the world.

When Maria Egipetovna threw open the door, the old man didn't fall down as was to be expected, but ran in, arms outstretched, like a decapitated rooster in that last second before keeling over and going into its death rattle.

Having run indoors, he collapsed on the homespun passage rug and fell asleep. He snored in his sleep, kept swearing, and bubbles of saliva burst at the corners of his mouth.

"You old bast . . ." said the old woman to him, when he came to. "You old sod, alcoholic, pissed again, shitbag . . ."

"Don't you shitbag me," replied the old man, sullen, but shy. "I wasn't drinking your money away, the boys treated me . . ."

"Ah-ah, the boys! When I go out, no one gives me a penny piece, but you get it handed to you day in day out."

"Well, who needs you, you old shlutch." The old man just couldn't get out the last word properly, so he had a second go: "Yeah, you old slut."

The old woman knew just how to cope with this. She let down her grey, scanty hair, which always clogged up her comb and stuck round the yellowy enamel wash basin, she started howling, yelling and keening; she went on about her youth and about how she regretted not getting married to Grigory Struev, a *nepman*, she beat her head against the cast iron knobs on the old bedstead, and her neighbour put on a vicuña wool headscarf and flew down the snow-covered path in the direction of the howls. "Oh, Maria Egipetovna, you poor woman, this is how the Lord rewards you . . ."

"What yer screaming for, what yer screaming for," said the old man slowly and gloomily. I ain't done anything bad to you, when have I ever knocked you about?"

"Yes you have, yes you have, of course you have," said Maria Egipetovna, rounding on him smartly.

"Well, I might have given you a lesson once, so what, it was only the once. You asked for it."

He waved his hand, spat and ambled off outside, because the

kindly neighbour had taken her in her arms and was whispering in her ear.

The old man slouched over the garden gate and dully eyed the sparkling snowflakes. The time had passed, long passed, when he was able to remember anything, or count on anything, or hope for anything.

Were he to lift his head, then he would see the moon, or maybe the man-made Luna satellite, etching the black sky with the tip of its antenna, but without catching on the stars.

But then he suddenly remembered that he had a bottle of Moskovskaya vodka stashed away, with about three hundred grams still left in it.

Disappearing into the snow drifts, he managed to reach the little shack in which they used to keep the cattle, in the days when they were allowed to keep cattle in the town, but which now accommodated sweet fuck all.

He burrowed into the snow drift like a dog, clamped his teeth on the neck of the bottle and started guzzling. Oh, it was good.

At first he started to feel sorry for his old woman. He went back into the house, subdued and sullen, rolled himself some baccy, but the old woman was up right away, her spirits raised, and catching the smell of fresh strong liquor on his breath, she started sounding off again.

"Shut up! Shut up!" he yelled back, pounding his fist on the table. You've made my life a misery, you old cow, all your squawking's enough to make me string myself up! I'll do it too. God damn you!"

"Go on then, go on then. What you waiting for? God damn you!"

And he stormed off outside again.The alcohol was coursing through his veins. He felt good. He tore down the washing line and set off towards the shack.

But when he had got everything fixed up: the noose, the stool, the hook – he went off the idea of dying.

"Na-ah," said the old man aloud.

He cut the rope into two pieces. He wound one piece round his waist, and he made a noose out of the other piece to go round his neck and he hung himself up on the wall, like a crumpled, tatty rag doll that had been lost and found several times over.

Yes, yes, you'd say that he hung there just like a rag doll in the midst of all that had gone on and was still going on all around him.

He hung there, all set to let his head loll on one side, stick out his tongue and bulge out his eyes as soon as he heard noise and footsteps.

He didn't have that long to wait. The old woman, whose heart stopped when she saw the open door of the shack, hesitated and stamped her feet, while her neighbour, consumed with curiosity, peeked into the darkness of the shack and let out such a shriek that half an hour later the engine of a three-wheeled police motor-cycle was roaring outside the house and above the racket, disappearing into the snow drifts there raced towards the shack, where various personages had already assembled, Detective Sergeant Lutovinov.

The ambulance hadn't yet arrived.

Gun in hand, a yellow pool of light from his police pocket torch, made in China, he peered into the distorted face of the suicide.

Undaunted and unwavering, the Detective Sergeant approached the corpse, and the corpse went and threw his arms round his neck, though, as I told you at the start of the story, nothing good came of it.

The policeman, poor man, took it bad, very bad. He was taken off to hospital in the ambulance that had arrived to collect the suicide. He was groaning and throwing up, they gave him injections and stuck a black mouth-piece connected to an oxygen bag between his teeth.

The old man was sentenced to fifteen days. Lutovinov himself, in a weak voice, had requested this of his comrades, when they, donning white hospital coats over their blue tunics, brought the patient chocolate, apples and oranges, which they'd paid for out of an official fund for the purpose.

The old man was sentenced to fifteen days.

During the day the old fella was taken out to break the ice on Peace Boulevard, and at night they locked him in the cells. He soon made two new pals. One kept singing: "She may be bent and hunchbacked, but she's rolling in money and that's why I love her, oh yeah . . ."

And the other kept lisping: "Tell me your game and I'll tell you your name!"

Maria Egipetovna paid him a visit once. She brought him some meat pies in a cellophane bag. She was really despondent, had gone sort of quiet, and felt sorry for him, but not too much. And now and then the old man would mumble to his new pals, as he licked his fag while they were having a smoke break: "It ain't right. I understand. I used to be educated. I understand everything. It was written in books – 'Merry-making in Old Russia'. I understand."

# The Electronic Accordion

"It's gonna be really nice back home now! Katya will be stirring up the borshch with her ladle. And the borshch will be as red as a banner. And what's the little darling going to prepare for the second course? If it's a bit of chicken . . . or mutton she's stewed . . . with fresh cabbage . . . a few potatoes in it, and tomatoes – that'll be great! But even if she's only fried up some eggs and salami, that'll be nice too. Jesus! How come a simple man like me can have such happiness? Little Vitya will grab me round the knees, shouting: "Dad! Dad! Let's get the building bricks and make a moon buggy to go to the moon!" He's growing up, the clever little devil, but he won't get spoilt for all that he's got. When we were his age we didn't live like him at all, no way. Never enough grub . . . just a bit of bread and salt to eat . . . Jesus! How come I've got all this happiness? All this just for me, just for a simple man like me!"

Such, roughly speaking, were the deliberations of one Pyotr Matveevich Palchikov, an honest man, a good, middle-ranking specialist, thirty-seven years old, and as you see, a family man, as he wended his way home after a stressful day at work.

And his home, like those of dozens of other manual and blue-collar families, was situated deep in the foothills of the Sayansky Mountains, on the right bank of the river E., a fair way from the centre of town, and as it turned out, from Pyotr Matveevich's place of work, whence he now betook himself by tram and bus.

The only inconvenience was this means of transport. Apart from this, in accordance with all the demands of present-day town-planning and construction, there was to be found in their district absolutely everything that the modern man required to lead a full-blooded and interesting life, replete in every respect.

Judge for yourself – in addition to the bathtubs in the houses – a large, splendid public baths was always steaming in the winter frost, complete with laundry and a dry-cleaning collection point, and don't even mention knitware, baker's, grocer's and fishmonger's shops – there they were, right under your nose. And not far away was the smart collective farm market with its reasonable prices, and for get-togethers and entertainment there was the club run by the rubber technical products factory, and there was even a pub in the district, while at the service of those who were keen on such things there was a real music school. Yes, you could live a thousand years in a district like this and never want to die!

Well, naturally enough, Pyotr Matveevich did not go to the pub. It was dirty and smoky in there, and people shouting. Drunks would pester you for twenty kopecks. And anyway, Pyotr Matveevich was not a great one for beer, though he had heard more than enough about its magical properties. They said it did this, and it did that . . . Bucked you up, got you going. Yet beer always made him want to doze off, when, in fact, Pyotr Matveevich always wanted to live, not sleep. So he'd picked up a quarter-litre of vodka in the shop. He walked through the darkening streets, the ice crunching underfoot, and yellow lights were already lit in the houses, and the blue mountains were already darkening and merging with the sky above.

He was taking his usual path, but it had been badly churned up by people's feet, and the mud, despite the ice, was still slippery in places.

Pyotr Matveevich stepped in it once, then a second time, then he swore and decided to encroach on the territory of the music school. An asphalt path ran right from the palings there to the palings on the other side. All you had to do was hop over the fence, and then you'd be home – there was his house, a stone's throw away.

Pyotr Matveevich himself did not in general encourage such trespassing on the school's territory. He enjoined his son Vitya in this respect and warned off Vitya's pals. "It's not nice, chaps," he urged them. "After all, you're grown-ups now, aren't you? The caretaker has put a lot of work in there. Go and play somewhere else, learn to respect other people's work, lads . . ."

He did not encourage it. But at the moment he was most anxious not to get his new brown half-length boots all covered in mud. "Over the boards and over the bricks," whispered Pyotr Matveevich. "You'll get home somehow," he hummed.

And though he was utterly absorbed in his cares about preserving his personal cleanliness, as well as in thoughts concerning his imminent family happiness, he suddenly saw that the school windows were illuminated in a way that was rather unnatural for that time of the evening: every single one of them was lit up, and brightly too. Usually at that time – well, there might be a light on here, or a couple there, where someone was scraping away on a fiddle, or thumping the piano, or opening their mouth wide, though you couldn't hear through the glass what sort of a song was pouring out of it.

In his curiosity Pyotr Matveevich pulled on his spectacles and discovered by the door the following handwritten text on a piece of white paper:

The electronic accordion
played by Kudzhepov
Works of the classics and by Soviet composers
tickets on sale

"Tickets on sale!" said Pyotr Matveevich slowly. And he spat angrily. "What a God-awful thing to think up – an electronic accordion! They've gone completely nuts!"

He condemned it, but he did not budge from the spot.

Because he had seen a lot of accordions in his life, and he had known an extraordinary number of concertinas, but an electronic accordion, now that was something that he just could not picture, no matter how he tried. And his swearing only inflamed his curiosity. So he decided to go in, so that, should the occasion arise, he would have an opinion on this subject too. As they say, it's better to see something once than to hear about it a hundred times. And in addition to that, he could describe this interesting phenomenon to his family afterwards, and discourse to his workmates on the practical use of it or its harmful effects. So Pyotr Matveevich decided to go in anyway, and sparing no expense, he made ready with a rouble note.

However, on entering the foyer, he saw in the first place that there were no tickets on sale at all, indeed no box office at all. And in the second place the sounds of organized human speech were issuing from behind a white door.

Pyotr Matveevich put his cap in his pocket, cautiously opened the door a crack, and then found himself in the back row of a small auditorium.

People looked at him absent-mindedly. No one asked to see his ticket, they just whispered "quiet" when he scraped his chair. Everyone was listening to the man standing on the stage.

"Thus, dear friends, the electronic accordion is a very interesting innovation in music. And we all hope that soon our industry will start mass production of these remarkable instruments, which at present we are purchasing from abroad, and unfortunately, comrades, only for hard currency." The speaker shook his mane. "So, comrades, the day is not so far away when a huge number of our listeners, our lovers of music, will delight in the deep sounds of this instrument, which, as I have already said, is, in its richness of tone, close to the organ and the clavichord, yet combines all this with compactness and requires no special performance skills."

This was, apparently, Kudzhepov himself. From a distance Pyotr Matveevich could not make out his face in detail. However, he could see that he was evidently a man not in the first flush of youth, with a receding hairline, his mane notwithstanding, wearing a black suit, rather dapper in appearance – well, that's how people like that are supposed to look.

And the accordion didn't look anything special. You couldn't see anything electronic about it either. Were there really wires running off into the wings? It was just an accordion like any other.

"Common trickster," grunted Pyotr Matveevich. "What a God-awful thing to think up!"

But while he was grumbling he missed what was being said. Because Kudzhepov said something else and then deftly extended the accordion's bellows.

Suddenly it got to him! Took hold of him, sent him spinning, carried him away, his heart was in his mouth, he was caught, shivers down his spine, it warmed him up – sweet weariness and giddiness. The tune, and the sweet pain, and youth and old age, all together!

"What's this?" whispered Pyotr Matveevich. "Wha-at is this?"

"Something you need to know, young man," said his neighbour with dignity, a shrivelled-up old woman, wearing glasses tied up with thread.

"I'm not talking about that. What's happening to me?" whispered Pyotr Matveevich.

"Stop bothering me while I'm listening!" said the old woman, losing her temper.

"I didn't mean anything," said Pyotr Matveevich in confusion.

And suddenly the tears started to stream silently down his cheeks, and he was ashamed of them, but still wept, in utter silence, while still looking straight in front. The little auditorium, the black-clad musician and his magical musical instrument all swam before his eyes. And the music swam and swam too.

Pyotr Matveevich felt for his handkerchief and suddenly found the quarter bottle of vodka. Such a sudden anger seized him that, to the profound amazement of his neighbour, he leapt up from his seat, stamped his feet, waved his hand absurdly, shouted something, and shot out onto the street like a bullet.

There was the same night outside, a streetlamp creaking in the wind, a steady light burning in the windows of the houses, everything around exuding night, quiet and tranquillity.

In his agitated state Pyotr Matveevich was on the point of smashing his bottle on the asphalt, but then changed his mind, his face grew darker, he pulled his cap determinedly over his eyes, and set off home, without picking and choosing his route.

"Jesus! Look at the state you're in, just like a pig! Your trousers all covered in mud," gasped his wife. "Where the hell have you been?"

Pyotr Matveevich took off his things without a word, but seething with rage.

"Have you been drinking with someone, or something?" said his wife, examining him.

At which point Pyotr Matveevich cracked.

"'Drinking'! 'Drinking'!" he yelled. "I'll give you 'drink'! All you can think of is drinking and stuffing yourself! You haven't got a thought in your head! You live like a carp under the ice! Are you going to drag me into the grave with you? Don't you know how other people live? What is there on television for you today? *Stierlitz*? Or Who?"

"It's *The Thibault Family*. France," said his wife, her voice trailing away. "We can eat now and watch it all afterwards."

"You fool!" shouted Pyotr Matveevich, filled his lungs with air and then repeated: "You fool! You fool!"

His wife gasped, while Vityua abandoned his moon buggy construction kit and retreated into a corner, sobbing: "Daddy! Daddy! What are you doing? Why are you telling Mummy off?"

"Clear off!" said his father, stamping his foot at him.

By now the son was crying fit to burst. Then Pyotr Matveevich more or less came to his senses, more or less returned to his old self. He looked slowly around. The house was still a house. The flat was still a flat. The furniture still furniture. The people still people.

"Well, actually . . . I . . . it was . . ." He rubbed his temple with his finger. "Katya, don't be angry with me. You get all wound up at that bloody job of mine, pulled every which way . . . We had it again today: they've allocated us funds for sheet aluminium, and when I get over to the stores, they tell me there isn't any. Real struggle to get it . . . they've been on at me all day, and you get yourself all worked up. And then I was going along past the music school – do you know what a God-awful thing they've thought up? A real circus turn this one – an electronic accordion, can you imagine that?!"

"Oh, you gave me such a fright, such a fright, you really are a performer yourself," said his wife, laughing with relief. "I thought to myself, he's drunk or something. Or he's gone round the twist, just like that Misha who worked as an assistant in our factory . . ."

Pyotr Matveevich laughed as well. They both laughed and slapped each other on their fleshy backs.

And only their little son Vitya looked on like a wolf cub. The tears on his cheeks had dried, but his lips were pressed tightly together.

# Sledges and Horses

At that time our street was still unpaved, or more precisely, it had been paved, but it had taken a long time. At first it wasn't paved, and then they covered it with ringing cobblestones, and then along came the asphalt rollers and the asphalt tubs started to bubble away. They smeared it all on, rolled it out, smoothed the street out, and in the winter even started to clear the snow away. That's the sort of developments that came about in our quiet little street.

And then it was summer. And in the summer there was the yellow and grey dust, which was raised by cart wheels, chickens and boys' feet.

The dust concealed little unseen slivers of glass, lacerating your heels, and globules formed, drops of dust. And the yellow and grey dust made your blood thicken, and at first there flowed dirty blood, and then it thickened, and then there was nothing at all, it all healed up tight.

Snow fell, and the sledge-runners churned it up right away, but it still didn't squeak. And a horse would keep its legs a bit to one side, because it was going fast: hot was the steam from the horse's mouth, and the spiral disappeared in the air. Now and then a one-and-a-half ton truck would go by or a ZIS, but more often than not – sledges and horses.

There were different kinds of sledges. My favourite one – the one from the municipal cleaning trust – carried square, wooden boxes. Inside them was the trash, the dirty snow, anything that wasn't needed, all being taken out of town. You just hung on the back – you couldn't be seen from up front, and it was comfortable. And you rode along like a postillion.

But the sledge marked BREAD and the sledge marked POST were no good at all. They were smooth, had iron locks all over them, and were cold.

And then there were the *rozvalni*, the low, wide sledges – neither one thing nor the other: you could get a ride on them all right, but if you were spotted, the driver would flay you alive with his whip.

The sledges and the horses I can still see, but the faces of the carters, the coachmen have all been obliterated. Completely. I can only remember a general outline. A half-length fur coat. A broad belt. Felt boots. A hat. Padded mittens.

There's only one mug, that of a young fellow, that still sticks in my mind. It keeps coming back to me, as vivid as if it were yesterday. Smirking, really nasty.

It was the big chief's sledge, he'd got it from the boss. It came round the corner smoothly and slowly, even though the horse was tetchy, kept jerking its head, chaffing at the bit. His master wound the reins round his hand, and the horse snorted "Khrrr-rr-rr", showing its yellow teeth, "Khrrr-rr-rr".

And the driver looked at me, and he knew that I was all set to act, I'd tensed my legs. And he knew that I would never touch his sledge in my life, because I had realized that he too had realized precisely what I was up to.

And then –

now this is what he looked like: he was wearing a Moskvichka coat – single-breasted, with a beaver-lamb collar, high felt boots stuck into the straw up to their tops, a good growth of hair sticking out from under his fur cap, and a face exuding strength, youth and good looks –

and then:

"Boy," he shouted, "You hang on, and I'll give you a ride, what d'ya say, lad! . . ."

And I kept quiet.

"Now don't be afraid, silly, hang on and we'll go for a ride right now."

So I hung on then, didn't I, silly me.

And then he let the horse have it with the whip.

And, wow, off we went! Me on the running board at the back, and he cocking his hat. He sang “Fly from the road, bird”.

And the speed made it feel as if the sledge wasn’t running along a smooth road, but over some kind of magic, undulating surface. Careering from side to side, and you had to lower your head – there was just a blur before your eyes, a snowy-grey blur. You couldn’t see anything.

“Fly,” he said, “from the road, bird . . .”

“Beast,” he said, “get off the road . . .”

And then he turned round and spat right in my – was it mug or face? I don’t even know what the word is when somebody has spat in it.

Well, I wiped myself, and on we went. Only now I was really upset, moping and miserable. I felt I had to jump off, but I was scared. And the driver, the bastard, wasn’t even looking at me. Not even a “Ha-ha-ha” or a “Hee-hee-hee”.

Then he turned round again and “gobbed” on me once more, and that’s what did for him, the idiot.

Because after the second time, I acquired the knack and I acquired the courage too.

I slithered off the sledge. I picked up a chunk of ice, threw it and hit the guy spot on. Full force. And I could see that I’d got him right on the bonce.

And the casualty put the brakes on, while I made a run for it under a gateway. Sent an old woman in my way flying into a snow drift, and with one jump I was on the other side of the fence. Just a coat flashing by. Firewood. A shed. Hide in the corner.

And I heard heavy, scraping steps, and grinding teeth, and coughing and swearing, but I was smart, quiet, motionless, and so I wasn’t found.

And when I’d sat out the siege, I came out onto that selfsame street of ours and I saw that there was snow, snow, fresh snowflakes were falling, and on the old snow, lumpy and yellowing, there were red stains. And the fresh snowflakes were covering them up, covering them up. Soon they would conceal it all.

# Teddy Boy Zhukov

*Teddy boy Zhukov was only a kid*
*But a pair of jeans was what he wore.*
*And all the birds that came his way*
*He dragged through the restaurant door.*
From the poetry of N. N. Fetisov

One nice Autumn evening in 1959 there was a do for the pupils at our school. All day long you could feel the heightened atmosphere at school: there was something really special about the way the bell rang, something really right when we answered the teachers' questions and even the caretaker woman, Fenya, was amazingly sober that morning.

And not surprising! After all, a party is a party. Everyone was really excited. The headteacher Zinaida Vonifantievna delivered an excited, but warm speech, and then the amateur concert began.

We sang Matusovsky and Bogoslovsky songs, performed scenes and sketches from Dykhovichny and Slobodsky, read poems by Mayakovsky, while I played a dance from Glinka's opera *Ivan Susanin* on the lead *domra*. The school's wind and light-entertainment orchestra accompanied me: accordion, trumpet, piano, doublebass. "Our Jazz" as we called it in whispers in the lobbies (i.e. the toilets).

"And now for the dancing!" proclaimed Zinaida Vonifantievna ceremoniously.

And it began – the spinning of waltz, the foot-stamping of the *gopak*, the graceful interplay of the quadrille. Everyone danced: Zinaida Vonifantievna herself partnered the physics teacher who was nicknamed Zavman, the director of studies Anastasia Grigorievna, all decked out in the fanciest lace, the young women teachers, who'd only just done their teacher's training, wearing long skirts, and even the Komsomol organizer Kostya Mochalkin, Mochalka-the-Sponge, in his Moskvichka jacket, with the steel cap of a "never-ending" pen poking out of its breast pocket. Cups of confetti showered down, there was a sack race and a blind man's buff game in which you had to cut off various sweets hung up on threads. Holding hands, we jokingly whirled in a gleeful circle around our favourite teachers.

Then suddenly everything went quiet.

Everything went quiet because teddy boy Zhukov had walked into the hall.

Teddy boy Zhukov was wearing a long jacket, his hair was done in a greasy quiff above his forehead, which was covered in pimples. Teddy boy Zhukov was holding two tarted up ladies with peroxide blonde hairdos by the elbow.

The threesome sidled over and seated itself on the chairs by the wall. Zhukov let go of his lady friends' elbows and hitched up his narrow, short trousers, beneath which glared a pair of synthetic, luminous, red socks.

Everything went quiet.

"Would you tell us, Zhukov, who let you in here looking like that?" asked Zinaida Vonifantievna in a loud voice.

"Old aunt Fenya let me in because I'm a pupil here," answered Zhukov quietly, looking at the floor.

"And who are these two . . . persons?" enquired Zavman sternly.

"They're Inna and Nonna. This is Inna, and this is Nonna," explained Zhukov, still abashed, "from the technical college."

"'Nonna'!" was all Zavman could croak.

"Well now, Sasha," said his young form mistress, addressing Zhukov with a wry smile, "Are your mummy and daddy happy about you going around looking like a monkey?"

At that Zhukov fell silent.

"Answer up, Zhukov! I think you're being asked a question, aren't you?!"

But Zhukov stayed silent.

"Now what's this all about, my friend? Mischievous as a kitten and scared as a rabbit?" said Zavman unpleasantly. And he took out his comb and combed his remaining hairs over the crown of his head.

But Zhukov still had nothing to say in reply. Whereupon, to everyone's surprise, his female friends spoke up, bold as brass.

"What yer getting at the bloke for!" hoarsely yelled right in the headmistress's face either Inna or Nonna, you couldn't tell which because they both looked exactly the same.

Zinaida Vonifantievna was struck dumb.

"'Mummy and daddy'! Right now mummy and daddy are rolling round in bed pissed 'cos they just got paid, and they're not going to give a monkey's about us. Ha-ha-ha!" said the other one gleefully.

"Oh, Good Lo-rd, good Lo-ord!" groaned the headmistress, glancing round in alarm at the pupils who had all crowded round. "Whatever goes on in these unfortunate families!"

"Good Lo-rd, good Lo-rd – don'tcha get bo-red?!," mumbled the first girl. And turning to Zhukov, she said: "Zhuk, come on Zhuk, let's get out of here, it's a real drag 'ere"

"Let's go," agreed Zhukov, and in full view of everyone kissed the girl who had eagerly proffered her red lips to him.

And off they went. And after this hitch, the fun and games not only continued, but even triumphed. We played "Postman's Knock" and "Sleeping Statues". I remember, I won a cardboard whistle.

But not everybody played. Behind the scenes, by the dusty backdrop with the picture of the collective farm worker carrying the sheaf of corn, and the steelworker in the felt hat and the cavalryman on horseback and the machine-gunner by his machine gun, there wept the Komsomol organizer of class 9a, Valya Kon. Wearing her neat little school uniform dress with its little white collar and the little apron, and with her ashen little curls and her freshly washed little face, and with a gold-coloured watch on her wrist, she wept in Zinaida Vonifantievna's arms, while repeating to her: "Oh, Zinaida Vonifantievna! Oh! There are a lot of good, clean, pure, things about him as well. He cuts things out with a fretsaw. He's got a puppy called Pal. There's no need to do this to him."

"You must understand, my girl," said Zinaida Vonifantievna, smiling wisely, "we usually resort to this only as an extreme measure. It is better to cut out the diseased organ immediately, than to let the rot spread further. It's healthier for the body and for the organ," said Zinaida Vonifantievna, smiling wisely.

Zavman was lurking nearby.

# Robber

Once Galibutaev showed up at home bearing a half-litre of vodka in the inside pocket of his sleeveless jacket.

Given today's prices for vodka and other strong drinks, the mere thought of them causes the drinking man to smile bitterly, of which fact Galibutaev informed his wife Mashka.

And the latter replied: "Don't you go chattering on so much, just sit down and we'll have some grub."

"Tut-tut, you robber," snapped Galibutaev sternly, and put the half-litre on the table. But he smiled.

And once he'd taken off his sleeveless jacket, yanked off his boots and unwound his footcloths, he set about having a wash.

And barefoot, washed, and wearing only his vest, he sat down at the table, on which there steamed the cabbage soup, while the vodka looked out of the glasses with lively eyes.

"Yes . . . Vodka." said Galibutaev, and took a drink.

And Mashka took a drink too.

"Now you say 'robber'. How many times do you have to be told not to talk like that. I'm a working woman," she starts up.

"I know. Galibutaev knows everything. I said 'robber' to you to put some life into you. Understand?"

"No, I don't," said the woman.

"Well learn, then. I want to see animate objects. An inanimate object is something I don't want to see and I can't bear the sight of. I want to see you animated, and that's why I called you 'a robber'. Understand?"

"To inspire me, or something?" asked Mashka uncertainly.

"No. To animate you. Do you understand?"

Mashka took offence.

"There's one thing I do understand. I understand that before long I'll chuck you and all your talk out of this flat. Clear off, clear off. You'll see what an animate object you've got here."

And being so upset, she drank down another half glass in one go.

Galibutaev fell deep into thought. And he had something to think about. The long and the short of it was that he didn't have a place of his own. And though Mashka was, of course, his wife, the marriage hadn't been registered. So she could ask him to make himself scarce at any moment.

"Well, don't get so upset,"said Galibutaev in a conciliatory tone.

"I'll throw you out, you know," promised Mashka. "As soon as the children come back I'll throw you out. Just you wait."

"Oh, the children," said Galibutaev, pouring out the rest of the bottle into the two glasses, and getting on with his dinner.

That was the problem, the children. Mashka had four of them, but the two daughters, thank God, had got married to two demobbed soldiers and gone off with them somewhere.

Then there was the son, Mishka – he was the biggest pain in the neck. He worked in the same factory as Galibutaev and was forever driving him up the wall. Either he was asking something dirty, or he was pushing him, or he would start making Galibutaev read the newspaper out to him, knowing that the latter was utterly incapable of reading the newspaper because of a severe squint and his near total illiteracy. He hounded him. Galibutaev was scared of this pain in the neck, but likewise gave no quarter. Each gave as good as he got.

But young little Seryozha – he was completely inoffensive, sort of, in view of his Young Pioneer age, but potentially he was also a threat to Galibutaev, to his love life and to his flat, since, as he was growing up a bit now, he was starting to feel ashamed of his mum's behaviour, of which the whole street knew.

After they had eaten, the couple's mood improved significantly and they turned on Mashka's television.

"In this instance the American bourgeois professor reveals his complete ignorance of the fundamentals of Marxism-Leninism," said the presenter.

And so on. And then there was a concert and a film called *A Stake Bigger than Life*, about the tireless Captain Kloss. After which the television closed down and went dead.

The day went dead too. The day closed down. The evening closed down too. Night fell, after which both Galibutaev and Mashka would again have to go out and earn money.

"Must get some cash together," said Galibutaev, stretching himself.

"Eh," said Mashka, not hearing, as she set about making up the bed.

"Cash, I said! Have you gone deaf!" yelled Galibutaev, and went out onto the porch.

It was night-time out on the porch as well. A full moon was shining. You could see the white sheds in the darkness. Almost all the windows in the barrack house had gone dark. It was night, and Galibutaev went back indoors, to bed. And once in bed he was lord and master of all he surveyed.

"Mashka, let me sort of rape you tonight," he said. Mashka's interest was caught.

"What do you mean exactly?"

"Well, just this. You sort of fight me off as hard as you can, like for real, and I'll try to screw you."

"Come on then," said Mashka gleefully.

. . . "And then I pounced on her like a ferocious beast," Galibutaev told me. "I ripped everything off her. And she was writhing, and she was scratching, and she was squealing . . . Any other rapist would have given up long before. But not Galibutaev. I ripped everything off her, and I was all set to do it when she sent me spinning, and I fell off the bed and hurt myself."

"What did you do?"

"I broke my big toe on my right foot. I landed on my toe." And Galibutaev swore long and hard.

"Well what happened then?"

"Just you listen."

. . . In the morning Galibutaev limped into work, called the foreman aside, and explained all the circumstances to him. The foreman didn't say anything, and they went off to do their work – unloading barrels of cucumbers.

The foreman came over and stood by Galibutaev where they were unloading, and ever so, ever so carefully, very cautiously lowered the edge of a barrel onto Galibutaev's foot. Though actually, it was on his left foot.

"Oh-oh-oh," said Galibutaev, yelling and screaming. "Oh, me poor foot, me dear old foot! Oh-oh-oh!"

After which they made out an accident report. Galibutaev went to the hospital, where they X-rayed his big toe. The X-ray fully confirmed an industrial injury, and Galibutaev was given a certificate of exemption from work on full pay.

And Galibutaev came home, where Mashka roared with laughter when he told her the whole story.

"So they're going to pay you money as well for all this business? That's nice."

". . . And I stayed at home for a whole month," Galibutaev related, his eyes shining. "I didn't lift a finger. And me and Mashka got up to all sorts of tricks, the like of which no one knows how to perform these days."

"And then what?"

"Then what? Then she chucked me out anyway. That sod Mishka came back from a business trip. Seryozha came home from Young Pioneer camp. She chucked me out, and cried. I can't go on like this, she says, and I can't go on any other way either. I've got children, after all. The robber. She broke my toe. Do you know how much she weighs? Ninety-six kilos. She's ten years older than me."

"That's not bad going!"

"No, not even ten," said Galibutaev, and started to work it out. "I'm thirty-two, and she's forty-three. So she must be eleven years older than me."

"She gave me everything," he said, continuing with the story of his unhappy love life. "She gave me everything that I could call my own, even her first husband's leather jacket. He was a technician at the aerodrome. Everything – my sleeveless jacket, and my work clothes, and my coat from East Germany, and my felt boots, and my hat. The only thing I left at her place was the tar."

"What tar's that?"

"The tar. I had a little bottle of tar, to coat my boots with. I left it at her place. I'll have to ask Mishka to fetch it for me, or I'll have to go round there myself."

"And where are you living now?"

"I'm not living anywhere now, I'm just dossing. I'm dossing here, in the garage. But I've been promised a room. Here at work. And it'll be winter soon. But I'm not afraid of winter at all, because she gave me everything, felt boots, and a hat. And the tricks we got up to – no one knows how to perform them these days. You know . . ."

And Galibutaev laughed joyfully.

And when he'd had a good laugh, he carried on.

"I'll tell you one thing. I've been severely short-sighted since I was a child. They used to call me squint-eyed because of that, and I only completed two years at school. Because I was unable to study. Oh! I was supposed to have had really careful teaching! Special lighting, at set times, and only if I was in the right mood. And what chance was there of getting all that, when I was being brought up in a children's home?"

"Was it bad in the children's home?"

"Why should it have been bad? I'm very fond of the place even now. They even took me to see the chief eye doctor, Filatov, but he only said that they'd brought me in too late, and he wanted to tear the medal off the director's jacket."

"What medal was that then?"

"How should I know? She had a medal on her jacket, and Filatov wanted to tear it off. You've ruined this boy, he said. But what was it to do with them? They took good care of me. Only they didn't know that I should have been taken to see Filatov right away.

"That's why I can only see animate objects. I can't bear the sight of an inanimate object. And an inanimate object is everything that is written down, and everything that is all around.

"And an animate object – that was my 'robber'," said Galibutaev, and he had no desire to carry on the conversation with me, reckoning that any further questions from me would be posed with the sole purpose of having a laugh at him.

# Mountains

A quiet man went out one evening to get some grub in the Kebab House on the corner of Zasukhin and Semenyuta Streets, a place which, to be fair, did not deserve such a high-falutin name, and ought to have been called, plain and honest, a "spit and sawdust place". For there were always dropouts hanging around there, hawkers from the bazaar, teddy boys, drunken workmen and other disgusting persons whom we couldn't possibly take with us into the approaching radiant future, which is not miles away beyond the mountains.

And well – the choice and quality of the food in this miserable establishment also left a great deal to be desired. Naturally, there wasn't even the sniff of a kebab, and the only thing they served was murky cabbage soup made of sauerkraut and some sort of run-of-the-mill "hake", criminally fried in some unidentifiable engine oil or something. Which was why an unbearable stench enveloped not only the catering outlet itself, but the whole surrounding area as well, which consisted of the wood and slag-built little houses of this big-city suburb. It was odd that the district health inspectorate hadn't got around to closing the disgusting breeding ground down and boarding it up good and proper! It was astonishing, and it testifies to the existence of certain shortcomings in that service too.

And our quiet man, Omikin by name, was in no way a seeker after entertainment there, he wasn't a black marketeer or an alcoholic, but simply a quiet citizen of the Russian Federation, abandoned by his wife for his timidity, and too lazy, as it was gone seven in the evening, to find anywhere else to eat, where, more specifically, the food might be more respectable. All the more so, (let's not beat about the bush!), all the more so, given that his income for the time being did not permit him, were he to be seated at a decent table in a smart restaurant, to consume something richer in calories and more delicate on the palate. His income . . . maybe it was also for this material reason that Omikin's beautiful wife had left him.

It had all happened like this. He and his wife were travelling from the city centre on an overcrowded bus, standing on the front platform, where suddenly a middle-aged juvenile delinquent, apparently drunk on vodka or high on hash he'd been smoking, started to get out of hand. Long-haired and unshaven, at first he just seemed to be dozing, squashed up against the door, but then he came to, spotted the beautiful Mrs Omikin, and said loudly: "Oy, Miss! Poetry, stars, do you know what all that is?"

Such an utterance struck the quiet Omikin as most unpleasant, and containing himself, he merely addressed his wife, reminding her that the next day was the 19th of the month, to wit the very day on which they had to collect the family wash from the laundry: sheets, underpants, pillowcases. The hooligan burst out laughing deliberately, and Omikin's wife, boiling over with incomprehensible anger, started, as it were, to detach herself from her husband, and she eventually succeeded at their stop, where, once they had alighted, she declared: "I do not want to live with a man who cannot defend me as a woman from the first hooligan he comes across who can't behave himself."

Mr Omikin sheepishly declared that the hooligan hadn't altogether misbehaved, and that maybe he wasn't even a hooligan at all, but some young undiscovered poet or inventor, at which his wife broke into long and contemptuous laughter.

"You coward! You toe-rag!" the woman hurled at him with a final guffaw. And shortly after that she left Omikin altogether. Because her new husband, an ex-widower – a trim figure, outward-going, gallant – worked as something in the military, had a dacha and a three-room flat, and was always going away on long business trips. So who would leave a remarkable husband like that and go back to her old one, even if she had loved him once, back to her ex- , who was a layabout, living in a grotty little wooden house, which was forever going to be demolished, but never was, who didn't have any wealth and never would, because that was his fate, he didn't have that kind of go in him! Who would go back to a husband like that! Obviously, only a complete idiot, and that was something that Mrs Omikin most certainly was not.

When she had got married to Omikin she had done some calculating of her own. Against the background of general and unbridled delinquency and loose behaviour all around her, she had been struck by his unusual mildness. To all the insults and misunderstandings that still occur in our not entirely perfect life he would respond with a disarming smile and a mild gesture. Only when people made him particularly hot under the collar, would he murmur: "You know, it's not nice to do that, you shouldn't do that, you should be ashamed of yourself."

And when it came to Mrs Omikin, in those days his fiancée, whose maiden name was Milyaev, he didn't just try it on crudely so as to have his evil way with her, he courted her for a long time just like they did in the old days, he took her to the planetarium and showed her the various planets, and only later, a lot later, did he say to her, as he stared at the steps in front of her hostel: "Do you know, Lyusya, I think I love you. Would you consent to become my wife?"

That's exactly what he said: "I LOVE YOU, WILL YOU CONSENT TO BECOME MY WIFE?"! What a weirdo! At first Lyusya wanted to burst out laughing and make some wisecrack, but then she looked into his agitated, as it were, clouded face, and she somehow lost any desire to laugh. She suddenly thought that though she did of course have other, more dashing, suitors, they were all sort of . . . horribly clever. At least this one wouldn't be guzzling vodka by the litre and dropping his trousers in other people's doorways. And anyway, she herself was cheesed off with making do in hostels. Especially as she and all her fellow students in her evening class at the technical college for light industry were about to be allocated their work placements . . .

"Of course, I'm not insisting on an immediate reply," he went on, somewhat hoarsely, registering her silence. "But we have got to know each other a bit now. Lyusenka. So I think you're in a position to understand the seriousness of my intentions."

Well, she soon gave her consent. Secretly, she placed all her hopes on her own determined character. "It's a good job HE's the one who's like that," she thought, even joyfully. "I'll be in charge of him, he's courteous enough, I'll be in charge of him, and together we'll show THEM!"

But they didn't show THEM anything. And anyway, how can you be in charge of a dollop of blancmange? It runs through your fingers. Omikin continued to do his job regularly at the economics research unit, earning his salary of one hundred and ten roubles, there was still no sign of his old house being demolished and them getting rehoused, and Lyusya Milyaev-Omikin, a graduate specialist, began to get very bored in her spare time. While Omikin sat in his soft slippers in front of the television and read some great big boring book or other, she too, having washed the supper dishes in water boiled on the electric hob, stared lethargically into the same old television, and was occasionally addressed by Omikin: "Well then, little mouse, do you want to go to beddy-byes?"

"Yeah," she would answer rudely for some reason.

"Oh, why ever didn't you say so before," said Omikin in fright. "Well then, make up the bed then, make up the bed, and I'll go into the kitchen and do a bit more reading."

And that was that. And having suffered for some time and got sick and tired of the 'beddy-byes' and 'the little mices', Lyusya finally rebelled in the aforementioned manner and packed Omikin in for good.

And what about Omikin? Of course the event gave him quite a turn. He even wept inconsolably like a baby, when she informed him of her decision and made him believe it.

"But you know, it's not nice to do something like this, Lyusenka, have I done something to offend you?" he sobbed.

"Oh, leave off, I've heard it all before," she said angrily, as she packed into a huge grey suitcase made of imitation leather, all her various bottles, jars, tubes, blouses and tops.

"Have I really been such a bad husband to you?" he said in bewilderment.

"Oh, leave it alone will you! Why keep going over it a hundred times when everything's already decided," she said hurriedly, knitting her fashionable, plucked eyebrows.

"I suppose it's my fault, I suppose in actual fact I didn't pay enough attention to you," he kept repeating.

Well, how can you talk to a man like that? How can you tell him that nobody, that none of your girlfriends, lives like this? Did you even once buy her some Arabian perfume, or a gold ring, or take her on a trip to Sochi or Yalta? You haven't got the money? Well you don't have to go out and steal, you can earn it if you don't know how to steal, instead of reading useless books or lounging in an armchair with, it must be said, the stupidest of expressions on your face.

"What are you thinking about now?" she had once asked him.

"Eh?" he said, coming to.

"I'm asking what you're dreaming about with that look of all sweetness and light on your face?"

"Me? Yes. You guessed. I've been dreaming," he said with a smile. "You know, I've been thinking about you and me and about the radiant new future, which these days is not miles away beyond the mountains. And you know, it may be just a sort of cliché, a trendy phrase 'not beyond the mountains', but I can, you know, I can envisage these mountains quite clearly, covered with a kind of magic, clean, uncluttered woodland, emerald mountains beyond which there is a quiet radiant future, where there is no noise or swearing, or pushing and shoving, no envy and no squalor. Where the houses are roofed with red tiles, and the paths are sprinkled with yellow sand. Where the verandas shine with warm light, and where you and I will walk arm in arm – eternally young, eternally happy, eternally tender. We will caress the quiet flowers, listen to beautiful music and the falling of the cedar cones, we will bathe in a blue, blue lake."

"And what are you doing to bring about this radiant future of ours?" she asked, shaking with anger.

"Why just ours?" he asked in astonishment. "It's for everybody. It's an objective process. I am just honestly doing my job, honestly working, trying to be an honest man in my everyday life."

"And how much do you get for your honesty?" she asked, no longer able to control herself.

"Well, don't we have enough?" he said with a smile. "We're fed and clothed, we have shoes on our feet."

And you might have thought that he didn't notice her anger at all. Or perhaps in actual fact he really didn't notice it.

And so she packed him in. Well who wouldn't pack in a fool like that? Eh? Answer the woman, if you've got the courage.

So she packed him in. And at first Omikin pined sorely. Once he even drank a hundred grams of vodka, but he didn't enjoy it. He grieved in bewilderment, stopped reading for a time, and for a time his television was turned off. He stayed in in the evenings, silent and alone, and mulled over everything – what could have offended her, what had failed to please her?

"I didn't, I didn't pay enough attention to her," he said to himself with a frown. "I didn't perceive that there was a living person there outside my books."

But gradually he calmed down somehow. He never experienced jealousy. The unknown military man remained a mythical figure for him. He just could not picture in his mind's eye Lyusya undressing, taking all her clothes off and lying down next to another man. That would be monstrous and absurd. He just couldn't contemplate it. And gradually, in his mind's eye, it was as if all that had happened had not happened for real, it was only temporary. How could it be otherwise? Who else would he stroll with there, beyond the mountains, through those happy groves, greeting the sunrise and bidding farewell to the sunset? And gradually his bitterness was expunged, and gradually his life once again was back on its usual track.

As before, gentle and efficient, he sat at his work, once a month he visited the grave of his parents, who were buried out of town in the distant cemetery of Badalyk. And he read and read, constantly, read his abstruse books, which themselves could not be blamed for his downfall, reducing him to the quietest of conditions. That couldn't be it! After all, other people read books, and just you look at them – sharp as knives! Greased lightning – no flies on them!

And – he was just having some grub in the Kebab House. And maybe that's where he went wrong. That's where you could find fault with him. He should have either taken up cudgels against the sub-standard Kebab House by complaining, or he should have overcome his laziness and patronized more respectable places, it's not so expensive if you don't go over the top. Or, when all's said and done, if you don't know how to cook yourself, you ought to have take-aways, to last, say, three days at a time. You know how convenient that is – you just take the saucepan out of the fridge, warm it up on the hob and you're always full.

But he went to the Kebab House. He kept on going there, kept at it until the dreadful incident occurred.

As always, the Kebab House in the evening was packed with no-holds-barred piss artists. Omikin looked through the menu fixed on the wall, saw all the usual things, paid and got a receipt at the till, counted his change carefully, and then set about finding a free seat.

A seat – where would you find a free seat? Over there, under the palm tree, people were knocking back their own vodka they'd smuggled in, elsewhere a guy was slumped over the table asleep, mug down, others were engaged in a game of chance involving a matchbox, there wasn't a free seat anywhere for Omikin.

So he was forced to put his tray of food on the free edge of a table belonging to two seriously drunk young people of hippy appearance, who were communicating secretively with each other, and whose plain black Diplomat briefcases, these days the primary and unmistakable hallmark of a clandestine dealer in scarce goods, were placed close to their legs.

"Is this free, gentlemen?" asked Omikin, just in case.

But they did not notice his question. They were enigmatically trying to agree on somewhere to go next, so Omikin off-loaded his food, took his tray to the table for used trays, and on the way at the same time picked up a bottle of Borzhom mineral water from the buffet. Which was not an overly difficult thing to do, since the serving woman in the buffet had by this time sold all of her daily quota of cheap red "plonk", and there remained on the mirrored shelves nothing but French cognac, around which swarmed, like moths round a flame, a crowd of drunks, scorching themselves on the price of it.

Omikin drank a glassful of the delicious water and tucked in to his supper, trying hard not to listen in on the private conversation being held by the two emaciated representatives of the younger generation, because the conversation they were holding was disgusting in the extreme.

One of the young men was a bit sharper than the other and kept smirking more and more, while the second, by contrast – a bit on the thick side to judge by appearances – kept frowning more and more as the conversation went on – he obviously needed some persuading.

"So let's shoot over there now, mate!" said the bright young man slyly. "Just shoot over there and really have a good time!"

"Well, yeah, you really kill yourself chasing a good time," responded his interlocutor despondently. "We didn't let him have those albums today . . ."

"So what, we'll let him have them tomorrow! Sure thing. As if I wouldn't rip off Drovyanoi to the tune of fifty kopecks for The Beatles and *Sergeant Pepper's Lonely Hearts Club Band*. You don't know me, pal!"

"Oh yes I do, but there's no real cash in it, and what's the point in moving? I am a gentleman, not some twopenny-halfpenny scrounger, for Christ's sake!"

"You what?" said the bright one in astonishment. "You obviously don't know Valka the Cheek, do you? As if she wouldn't push a bottle my way if she's got the cash. I'll just hang around, hang around for a bit. The Cheek! You know the Cheek's a real goer, don't you?" whispered the young man, glancing round lasciviously.

"How disgusting," thought Omikin squeamishly. "No, we really must do something about our young people. "Albums", "cash" – this kind of sloppiness conceals something rotten to the core, we must do something, we definitely must do something about this sort of thing."

"And what a goer!" exclaimed the young man exultantly. "Yeah, she's all woman all right, even if she was born in 1942!"

"Who is she?" asked the thick young man.

"God only knows who she is. She's got some husband somewhere, old guy, some big-shot. Always shooting off on business somewhere."

"Has she got a girl friend," asked the sullen one directly.

"Good Lord, how disgusting," thought Omikin again, and gulped down the rest of his Borzhom water.

"She's set up a whole whorehouse there," said the young man, getting more and more excited. "Last time I took some photos. Do you want to have a look? It's what I call really graphic."

And with trembling hands he reached into his briefcase and pulled out a black envelope."

"Cor, don't they go!" said his interlocutor in astonishment. "Those birds really go, don't they!"

And one of the photographs fell out of the envelope. It fell to the left of Omikin, so that he could not help glancing at it out of the corner of his eye.

And – he died! Bleary-eyed, drunk, stark naked, it was HER, sprawling on a bed that had seen quite a struggle, her legs parted obscenely.

"Good Lord!" groaned Omikin, reaching for the photograph.

But the young man beat him to it. He snatched the photograph out from under Omikin's palm before you could blink and said coarsely: "Piss off, baldy, you old goat! Who asked you to poke your nose in? Piss off, no one's talking to you, just sit there, shitbag, and eat your dinner, get on with your grub!"

"Smash his head in," advised the sullen young man.

"That's Lyusya, Lyusya my wife!" groaned Omikin.

"Or let me smash him one," said the sullen one.

But regaining his good humour, the one making all the running put a stop to any fisticuffs.

"What are you blathering on about, old-timer? You what? Go on then, take it, take it – have a look, if you wanna, if you really wanna," he said, winking to his sidekick.

With trembling fingers Omikin took the photograph. And sure enough – there was that same dirty picture, the same dirty woman lying there, only it wasn't Lyusya at all.

"It's the Cheek, her very self!" said the young man, beaming. "So then, old-timer, obviously you're shit scared, 'cos that's the end of your family hearth and home. You owe me one," he said, addressing Omikin.

The latter suddenly came over all weak, sat back with his legs out-stretched, took a deep breath, and vomited uncontrollably. Whether the Borzhom had done its job, or whether the quality of the food in the Kebab House had finally hit zero, whatever it was, he puked up uncontrollably: straight onto the horrible plates and the table all covered in spit.

"Oy, what's all this, what's all this?", said the young man, recoiling.

And he hiccupped, his body shook, his stomach turned over, his head swam, and the exertion even made him emit a pungent indecent noise.

"Someone chuck him out of here, the skunk!", shouted some drunken on-looker.

"But he's not a drinker," said the woman who ran the buffet.

"Whether he's a drinker or not, why should we put up with the stink?" reasoned the drunk.

"Well, maybe he's ill," interceded the woman. "Aren't you well, comrade?"

Omikin raised his clouded eyes.

"There's no need to chuck me out, I'll go by myself," he muttered. "No need, I'll go by myself."

And he got up, but suddenly drew himself up to his full ludicrous height and screamed: "I'm going, but you can all stay here, and fuck the lot of you!"

The drunks laughed.

"You said he wasn't a drinker."

"Well, I'm not so sure now," said the buffet woman doubtfully.

But Omikin's strength had gone by now, he staggered, wiping away the sweat pouring down his face with a grubby handkerchief.

"I'm sorry, I know it's not nice to do this sort of thing, I ought to be ashamed of myself, one shouldn't do this sort of thing, I am sorry . . ."

"Just you go along now, just leave here nice and quiet like," said the woman kindly.

But Omikin couldn't hear her. He just doubled up, squatted down, swayed about and slowly rolled over onto his right side.

And – died. This time for good.

# The Singing of the Brass

On 29 February, leap year, he walked along the street where he lived, the black snow piled up along the pavements, he walked along and, with half closed eyes, he listened to and heard the cloying and beautiful singing of the brass instruments in the marching band.

In the open car – all in black and red, in red calico and velvet – travelled his father in an absurd horizontal position, seeing nothing with his closed eyes, seeing nothing, travelling along, but not even travelling, but rather being transported to the cemetery to be buried in the cold, black earth.

He was the son, and he was taking his mother on his arm, walking over the cobblestones, most of which had worked loose, taking her, his arm linked in hers, holding on tight to the sleeve of her threadbare gabardine coat.

There were no tears in their eyes as they walked, and many others followed them, and several of these were weeping, but there were no tears in their eyes either, because they had already shed their tears, and a person isn't a divine machine that can just produce tears, and so there were no tears in their eyes as they walked, and from time to time the son met his mother's gaze, and it seemed strange to him that a white smile rested quietly on his mother's white lips, and this made him feel that something was wrong somehow, and he kept telling himself that the expression on his mother's face was just his imagination, because it couldn't be right.

And in front of them the car was decked out in, decked out in rugs, flowers, velvet and red calico, and so the coffin in which his father lay looked ugly and even a bit grubby.

And all the time he was miles away, thinking.

He thought – why have so many people, why have so very many people gathered here simply to go along and bury his father's dead body in the frozen February earth?

They were going along, and they would get there, and they would bury it, and it would lie there alone until the spring and summer followed on after February, and then worms would crawl up to it, and they would suck the dead meat of his father's body, and water would flow and be filtered through it, and underground beetles and maggots would crawl through it, and it would itself start turning into soil, and would soon become – oh, yes it would – soil.

And all the time he was miles away, thinking.

Perhaps a funeral was an opportunity? An opportunity, an opportunity, an opportunity once again to prove, to prove that we will all go there, we will all go there, and that it is a mystery, a mysterious joy for a living person to be standing for a while by a yawning, open grave, throwing in a handful of earth, and yet still feeling that he's still alive, he's still alive, alive, alive.

And there is only the sweet and cloying, the neutral singing of the brass between the living and the dead, the singing of the brass which you can hear, those sobbing trumpets, your eyes half closed – and, when you listen, there is nothing else in the world, apart from the singing of the brass, the singing of the brass.

And they went on and on and on, and a hard and dry February snow began to fall, and his mother's grey headscarf turned white, and the snow on the face of the deceased did not melt.

They walked sullenly behind the coffin which had now turned white, behind the whitening wreaths, the whitening calico, the whitening velvet. And it didn't seem to them at all that they were burying themselves. No. Unspeaking and quiet they walked on, the coffin with his father's body in front of them, while behind were the crowd and the brass instruments of the march band.

And the snow storm would engulf them, they would vanish in the storm, and they would turn as white as could be.

They were being obliterated in the thick of the snow, they

were being washed away in the thick of the snow, and only the singing of the brass, cloying and beautiful and sobbing, still turned your soul, turned your soul inside out, and caused universal pain.

# Cat Catovich

One nice warm August night they were sitting in the stuffy kitchen near the bathroom, at a table covered with coloured oilcloth, facing each other.

"It's terrible how the ways of the Lord are unknown to man!" said Garigozov. "Terrible! People today have got so shaken about that they've lost their outlines, just like when you vibrate something. It's just, it's just, do you understand? It's just tough, you know! It's awful! Would I, for example, really have thought that she would do something like that?" complained Garigozov, who had been educated in the local polytechnic, to his friend Kankrin, who had been educated in the same institute.

Kankrin studiously stayed as quiet as quiet could be, and then sniffed and replied: "I agree with you completely, mate. Just you look here, right now, here's one specific instance, one example: outside it's the month of August and they've gone and turned the radiators on. Is it hot? Course it is. Is it stuffy? Course it is. And why? No reason. If it's stuffy, so what. And when it's winter, you wait and see when it's winter. When it's winter, mate, when it's winter and it's blowing a gale and we start getting snow drifts, then you'll be buggered if you expect them to turn the central heating up full. You see for yourself – it's either a sheer bloody waste of energy resources, or it's, or it's – altogether it's . . . God only knows what it is altogether!"

"You've posed the question correctly," said Garigozov approvingly. "You've put it correctly, though in a very specific way. Now just you try to understand, and I don't think that you'll disagree with me much over this. Just try to understand that after all, we OURSELVES are to blame for a lot. Understand? Because a lot of things are literally easy to put right, but you just have to avoid getting shaken about and vibrating, but somehow or other just take yourself in hand or something, you understand. Feel yourself, you understand, to be the master of your own fate, your own family, your own work, your own country finally! Understand?"

"Right, well, shall I pour the rest out then?" said Kankrin.

"Uh-huh," said Garigozov.

And the last of the white vodka went babbling and gurgling into the green glasses. And the friends drank it and grunted with satisfaction, sniffed the individual crusts of black bread and fixed their lively shining eyes on one another.

But – they kept silent. In this silence, arising not from deficiency but from abundance, there also passed a modest amount of double human time. Until some new sounds introduced themselves into the tap-dripping quiet of the kitchen: a variety of cautious scratch-scratching, shuffling, rustling noises and even definite rumbling noises.

"Was that you?" said Garigozov, coming to. "Are you hungry?"

"No, I'm not hungry," replied Kankrin tensely, pricking up his ears and tilting his head on one side towards the floor, in the direction of the finely carved sideboard.

"I'm telling you," prattled Garigozov inopportunely. "I'm telling you, that it's high time that the individual in today's world, who's all shaken about, a person who's completely lost his outlines, spared a thought for his soul, his soul."

"Yes," said Kankrin.

"And today's world has completely lost its outlines too," moaned Garigozov. Now it would immediately be clear to any newcomer on the scene who looked at him, that it was simply the case that his share of the drink had gone straight to his head and that all of a sudden he was pissed, as sometimes happens in the quiet of the night when one strikes up a close acquaintance with strong drink.

"Right then," said Garigozov, summing up.

But Kankrin was no longer listening to him. Kankrin suddenly pounced, lunged out, and dragged out from under the carved sideboard a poor cat of huge proportions, struggling and offering every resistance. The horrible fur of the guilty animal was standing on end, its pupil was huge and blazed with malice.

"He's been rolling a tomato about!" announced Kankrin excitedly. "See, there was a tomato rolling around under the sideboard. It was Va-aska the cat who was doing it," he sang out. "Va-aska the cat! Vaska needs a good hiding!"

"Yes . . . eh . . . he deserves a good hiding," agreed Garigozov, cracking his fingers squeamishly. "It's night-time, it's nice and quiet, we're having a conversation, and here he is . . .'

And Garigozov waved his podgy little hand in distress.

"Oh, you. Vaska-Vaska! Vaska, here, pussy-pussy!" said Kankrin, feeling more and more cheerful for some unknown reason. "Vaska, here, pussy-pussy! Vaska needs a good hiding!" he kept repeating.

And on hearing how his lonely fate was to be so bitterly decided, the tormented Vasily promptly closed his yellow eyes heroically and without a murmur prepared himself for torture. Now I'm not going to make so bold as to confirm it, but all the signs were that they would have punished him, maybe only lightly, but the drunken friends would have given him a thrashing, if . . . if the following hadn't happened.

What happened was that there suddenly appeared in the kitchen doorway the stern figure of a strapping, curly-headed, well-proportioned child, wearing black sateen shorts and the full uniform of a Young Pioneer, comprising a white shirt and a red scarf. The child said nothing for some time, but just stared piercingly into the crimson faces of the merry-making drinking companions. Then he cleared his throat.

"Pashka? Well – hello there! What are you up to, son, can't you sleep? When I was your age I was always asleep at this time. And you've still got your scarf on! Just look what an important person you are in the middle of the night!" said Kankrin with cheerful good-nature.

"My little son joined the Young Pioneers the day before yesterday, and he can't bear to part with the uniform," explained a flattered Garigozov, and then jokingly ordered: "Now then, be prepared, the day is done, the land of nod, off to bed you little sod!"

And at that point, to Kankrin's horror, the boy exclaimed in a little voice ringing with pent-up emotion: "Stop shouting, Dad! I'm not going to say anything now about you and Uncle Kankrin carrying on like this so that you might wake up Mummy, who's very tired after her work. But I will say that you mustn't even think of giving our pussy cat a good hiding. I love our pussy Vasenka and I'll fight for him. You're grown-up people, you play an active part in building society and you ought to know that you mustn't do things like that! You mustn't lose your moral bearings! You mustn't beat cats, or hit rabbits, or throw stones at birds!'

And with utter dignity he tore the cat out of Kankrin's hands.

"Oh you, oh you . . . Oh, why are you sounding off?" said Garigozov, turning pale. "Why are you sounding off? Why mustn't you? And is it all right to torture human beings then?'

And at this point Garigozov also jumped up and let fly at the child with a hail of imprecations, to which the Young Pioneer, with utter dignity, made no reply, but merely continued to stare proudly, boldly and honestly, while clutching the cat close to his heart and his Young Pioneer's scarf.

And there they stood, stock still, like a group of statues. And no one knows how it would have ended, if the floor boards hadn't started creaking and a sleepy-eyed, plump, jolly woman, middled-aged and wearing only a night dress, hadn't burst into the kitchen. She screwed up her eyes at the bright light and looked short-sightedly around at those present.

"And what are you making this racket for in the middle of the night, comrades?" she said in a sing-song voice. "Pashka! Quick march, you little rascal, off to bed, fast as you can! As for you, Egor, you're not behaving properly, causing all these disturbances," she said, turning to Kankrin. "I'm not objecting to you drinking the odd bottle, but there's no point in you creating disturbances, getting both Andryusha and yourself all worked up. Fine friend you are to him, you'll be really pleased with yourself, if he ends up in the madhouse again?"

"They wanted to beat the cat," announced the boy.

"The ca-at? Well you really are the limit!" said the woman, and burst out laughing. "No, this time the pair of you are really going to land up in the nuthouse. And another thing – Andrei! Andryush-ka! Do you remember what you promised me and Pavlik? Do you remember, eh? That you'd give up dri-inking!"

"What are you creating such a song and dance for?" said Garigozov, angrily. "What nuthouse? You leave the nuthouse out of it, I know what you want me in the nuthouse for! Doctor Tsarkov-Kolomensky said that you have to slow alcoholism down gently, not break it off suddenly when it's going full pelt. We had a couple of bottles, so we drank them. And we're going to give the cat a good hiding, because he was rolling the tomato around. And I'm going to give Pavlik a thrashing too, because he shouldn't talk to his own father like that. And I'm going to smash your face in because when I was in hospital, you were knocking around with a waiter from The North. Are you going to tell me that's not so?"

"Of course it's not so," said the woman in sincere disagreement. "Seryozha and I are just acquaintances. Incidentally, he's a married man. Pavlik loves you. And what about the cat? What do you want to beat that cat for?" asked the woman in astonishment. "There's no reason at all to beat it! Instead, let's tie a lovely red ribbon round it's neck and all do a nice dance round it!"

Garigozov and Kankrin froze, their mouths wide open.

"Ooh, Mummy too!' said the boy in delight. "Looks like she's put away two or three hundred grams of vodka with uncle Seryozha! . . ."

"Shh!" said Evdokia Apraxievna, sternly, but at the same time jokingly, for by now she had deftly decked Vasily the cat out in the aforementioned garment. The cat was hissing, but later on, once it had been bought off with a saucer of milk, it started deftly lapping at the said milk.

And taking hold of each other's hands, there in the night, in the quiet kitchen, they began to whirl around the animal as it gorged itself. Mum started singing:

*Let's sing, let's sing*
*About Cat Catovich . . .*

*Yeah, about Cat Catovich,*
*Yeah, about Cat Petrovich,*

sang Garigozov, Kankrin and the representative of the future generation in response to her.

And they danced quietly there in the night, in the quiet kitchen, around the animal as it gorged itself, those quiet people in this huge country. They felt empty, they felt stuffy, they felt good, they felt joyful. Kankrin started a folk dance. Garigozov stamped his foot.

"Come on, tell the truth, you old cow! Did you sleep with that waiter or not?"

"Quiet," said the boy. "Quiet, or the neighbours underneath will be banging on their ceiling with the mop."

"And we'll give them what for!" said Garigozov.

And it was night, and the street lights went out. Stumbling, Garigozov accompanied Kankrin through the dark entrance hall.

"Isn't life empty, mate!" he whispered hoarsely. "Isn't li-ife empty, mate! Why ever did we bother to go to university?"

But Kankrin didn't agree with him and furnished, in his verbal responses to this, numerous examples in support of his arguments.

# Why You're Always Broke

"Really? So what then? Well, I'm drunk. I'm sorry, but did you give me a drop? Right then. Well, what have I done to you? I was rolling about and trod on your foot? Oh, no, I didn't do it deliberately . . . I'm sorry, I'm sorry, I just dozed off. I was waiting for a train. I'm waiting for the local train out to Kubekovaya. I am sorry. It's not just because I'm drunk, I was asleep, but I'm awake now, I am sorry, I didn't mean you any harm."

A commonplace scene in Russia, dear to the heart. A guy wearing a crumpled hat and crumpled trousers, who has woken up in a suburban line railway station waiting room. His neighbour, an intellectual type, maintaining a fastidious silence in response to the erstwhile drunk's outpourings. Women, guys, girls and their long-haired blokes with their transistor radios, cracking sunflower seeds and occasionally yelling out in metaphysical rapture: "Well, I've had enough of you! . ."

And then the waiting room itself – with its famous Ministry of Transport hard benches, the age-old smell of carbolic, the potted "rubber plant" of mighty proportions, which – along with the picture of even greater proportions depicting scenes from the life of the leaders of the international proletariat – was supposed, according to the cunning design of the station management, to exert an aesthetic effect on the unruly passengers, soothe their passions, soothe their savage breasts.

"Yes! It was all the fault of that meat pie," said old crumpled hat, though his neatly turned out neighbour, with his nose stuck in a copy of *Pravda* turned away, and let it be known by his every gesture and expression, that it was only by virtue of his standing in life and his good nature that he wasn't grabbing the degenerate firmly by the collar and shoving him out the big doors, or even hitting him on the back of his scrawny neck with a hefty fist.

"It was the pie, the pie," the man who had just woken up kept repeating. "If it hadn't been for that pie, then maybe it might have all turned out different, mightn't it?"

The enquirer fell deep in thought.

"Though . . . the devil only knows, the devil only knows," he mumbled.

"Hey! Big Boots, what yer getting so worked up about? 'Ave yer got a fag?" a tall lad with a guitar called out to him.

"'Course I have!" said "Big Boots" reasonably.

"Comrades!!" the cultivated man was about to say, tearing himself away from his newspaper – but, on seeing the stern forehead belonging to the popular music enthusiast as he squatted on his haunches and, his huge arm, stretched out for a North *papirosa*, and tattooed with recollections of that same distant part of the world, the North, he merely exhaled a little breath, and then fastidiously inhaled, endeavouring to avoid the tobacco smoke of those cheap, filthy *papirosy*, poisonous both to his own personal health and likewise to that of other toiling people.

"Right then, tell me, what were you gabbing on about?" asked the staunch young smoker, addressing the older comrade absent-mindedly.

"Well look, I'm telling you about it. This pie was the ruin of me, and they'd given me my very last chance."

"What pie are you on about and what 'last chance'?" yelled the impatient young man. "Go on, tell me. Or are you just stringing me along? Eh?"

"I'm just getting going and you start butting in!" said the old man in irritation. "If you want to know, then listen. If you don't want to, then get lost!"

"All right, I'm listening," said the young man.

And the old man's tale poured out in a steady stream.

"Well. It began in the harsh years of the 1960s. Finding myself at that time with a responsible job and a good salary working in the supply industry, I overstepped the mark, and dizzy with success, started to drink cognac and pure spirit heavily, because they were a bit cheaper then than they are now, and I always had more than enough money.

"Well. Both my comrades and the management kept on warning me that sooner or later I'd land in the shit, carrying on like that, but I refused point blank to believe them, because I always did well at work, and that makes you weak.

"But time would tell that they were right. For because of my drunkenness I started having various setbacks at work, not to mention in my personal life, since soon after all these incidents, my wife left me altogether. And then awful things at work just came along thick and fast one after the other, like devils. For one thing, one night, drunk, I was crashing out on a bench, just like this one, at Savelovsky Station in the city of Moscow, because I couldn't find a hotel, when some unknown rats and skunks stole off me a skein of silver wire belonging to the State, which I'd been sent by aeroplane to fetch from the city of Syzran, since our workshop was at a standstill because of a lack of this wire, and they stole it off me. You yourself know what happens to you for that . . ."

"I understand," said the lad.

"Well, it's as plain as the nose on your face what I had to pay for that. Though they'd broken the rules as well. They had no right to send me to fetch that wire. The wire should have been dispatched by special delivery, because it was silver. But I didn't raise too many objections about it – they had other things on me.

"So well then. That was how, before I knew it, a little while ago, I'm standing under the steely gaze of Gerasimchuk, and he says to me: 'Well, Ivan Andreich, this is your last chance to go on working in our firm. And if you waste it – then we're just going to have to let you go, because even though some of your work is quite good, we've had more than enough of your escapades, and we're up to our necks in letters concerning you and requests to punish you, which we have been doing very mildly. So this is your last chance! Our contract with the greenhouse market gardeners runs out soon, and if they don't renew it, then that bloody German Metzel will say we're in breach. And we'll be paying out five thousand. That German will give us the boot right away, because he's a non-Russian and he doesn't want to understand any kind of business practice other than his own. And moreover, he's a very angry man: he has greenhouses, and all sorts of bastards with under-the-counter order forms from highly placed organizations come scrounging to him for onions, cucumbers, tomatoes, and radishes. And seeing as the orders come from high up, that German has to fulfil them even if it breaks his heart, otherwise they'd give him the sack. And he fulfils them, frittering away his German greenhouse property, and that's what's made him so bad-tempered, and you can see right away that he's bound to rip us off to the tune of five thousand . . .'

"'So what must I do then?' I ask, trembling in speculation.

"'What you have to do,' grinned Gerasimchuk, bold as brass, 'is get him to PROLONG our contract for six months, and then we won't have to pay five thousand.'

"'What does "prolong" mean?' I ask, my heart in my mouth, and speculating once again.

"'It means, my dear chap, get him to put back the DEADLINE,' says Gerasimchuk, still with the same grin. 'And then we won't be paying five thousand.'

"'What, do you think he's stupid or something?' I erupted. 'Why will he extend the contract if he knows that he can get five thousand off us?'

"'That's why we're sending you,' the devil says sweetly. 'This is your last chance to go on working for our firm. If you succeed, you'll be a star, a king, you'll get a bonus, and all your past misdemeanours will be forgotten. If you don't succeed – well, you yourself understand,' he said, spreading his hands in a gesture of sorrow.

"'You mean, just like in a fairy tale, is that it?' I asked quietly.

"'Yes, just like in a fairy tale,' confirmed Gerasimchuk. And I walked out of his office just as quietly, having made up my mind then and there to go nowhere anymore.

"Because for me to go there was a complete waste of time. For I knew that German inside out, just as he knew me. It was

I who had agreed the above mentioned contract with him regarding the delivery of our product. At the time the German was most unwilling to sign it, but I vowed and I swore that we would complete the work on time with the highest degree of exactitude and expedition.

"So there was nothing to be gained by my paying a friendly visit to the Kraut, except that he would have me thrown out, which is why I went over to the stand outside the labour exchange to look for a new job.

"Well, I saw there were 'Situations Vacant' everywhere, but I thought to myself – to hell with it, I'll take a ride over there, maybe it'll work out all right somehow: perhaps this German's suddenly gone off his head and he'll sign a new contract for me right away, and laugh his head off. I've got nothing to lose.

"Such were my thoughts when I entered that under-the-counter model farm. And proudly throwing back my bald head, I made my way between the rows of warm glass greenhouses with their interior lighting, full of cucumbers, onions and tomatoes for the bosses. After which I found myself in a little office, where, without stopping and not giving her time to catch her breath, I asked the secretary, insolent from the constant stream of petitioners: 'Is Vladimir Adolfovich in?'

"'Yes, he is,' she answered rudely.

"'I'll just go in and . . .'

"'Just a minute!' she howled, but I had already taken a step, opened the leather-clad door and seen that there was a bit of a meeting in progress. I was being harangued by some guy, but it was most certainly not my friend, bold kamarad Metzel, but an altogether different little fellow who was acting the boss.

"'Sorry for interrupting,' I said.

"And I took a step back.

"And that's where the secretary Ninka pounced on me, asking me where did I think I was going, and saying that Metzel really was IN, but in AT HOME, because he had retired a month ago and was now staying at home, offended that he had been given the push.

"'And if you're after onions or cucumbers, then we haven't got any, we won't get them till March or April, as we've only just finished planting them,' Ninka said to me.

"'My dear Ninochka,' I answered, 'What do I need your cucumbers for, my darling, when I've come to see you on a completely different matter, closely connected with production, and not to scoff everything or fritter it away.'

"'Well, that's a different kettle of fish,' said Ninka, calming down, and went on: 'You just wait a bit, he's got some comrades from Norilsk with him just now. They'll soon be finished and then he'll see you.'

"'Oh, I'll wait, I'll wait,' I replied. And I thought to myself: 'Jesus Christ, am I saved?'

"Well, I waited for about an hour and a half altogether. Then they all came out of there, all hot and sweaty as if they'd been in a steam bath. I said to the one who did the talking: 'Comrade! Comrade!'

"'What? No!' he barked. 'What do you want me for? We're going off to lunch. We haven't got any onions, we haven't got any cucumbers, we haven't got any tomatoes!'

"'But I . . .'

"'No onions! No cucumbers! Stop this criminal activity, understand! What have you got? A letter? Who from?'

"And he took the document I had in his own two hands and looked at it for a long time, making no sense of it at all.

"And then the clever little Ninka, just to show how clever she was, said to him with a giggle: 'Oh, no, Multyk Dzhangazievich, he's here on a different matter altogether. It's to do with extending the contract for the delivery of . . .'

"'Ah-ha,' said the new boss, mollified. 'Why didn't you tell me in the first place?'

"He took out his ball point pen, and my heart skipped a beat.

"'Where have I got to sign? Anyway, how come, comrades, you're letting us down over these deadlines?' he said to me reprovingly, holding both my document and his pen.

"'Well, we . . . we're reorganizing. It's only to be put back six months,' I babbled.

"I looked at him – oh, Jesus Christ! – how business-like was this remarkable man, how handsome was this fine fellow, standing there like a Caucasian rock, standing guard over the state's cucumbers and onions, promptly signing my piece of paper, and saying to Ninka: 'Put the official stamp on it. We're just off to lunch.'

"After which he went off with the Norilskians, who were impatiently pawing the ground like horses which had been stabled too long.

"And – oh, Jesus Christ! – I was saved! Ninka, all make-up and still giggling, put the stamp on it for me, I gave her a box of Pushkin's Fairy Tales chocolates that I had all ready, and indeed, just like in a fairy tale, on wings of joy and triumph, I flew out the door, away from that neurotic firm.

"Saved, I thought. Saved! I'll get a rise, I'll get a bonus, and all my past misdemeanours will be forgotten!

"And at that moment the phone went in the office. I hid behind the door.

"'Yes, yes. No, no,' said Ninka. 'He's just gone, just a minute – I'll have a look.'

"She ran out. I was hiding behind the door.

"'Comrade! Comrade!' she shouted down the stairwell.

"Ha-ha! No comrades for you today!

"She went back, deflated, and spoke into the telephone: 'No, it looks as if he's already gone.'

"Swearing in a foreign accent came out the phone, and you could even hear it on the other side of the door.

"Aha, I thought. Has he tumbled to it? Well it's a bit late now, brother. I've got a signature and an official stamp over it too.

"And I flew off on those aforementioned wings. A bright sun was shining, greetings, fair country! The sky was blue, it would soon be spring, there was already a warm breeze, and hadn't I done well! I'd looked after all my own interests and those of my dear old firm as well.

"The only thing was, I really felt like some grub, it was just two o'clock. I looked here, there and everywhere, but couldn't find anything to eat. Because everywhere was closed for lunch between two and three, and where it wasn't, there were queues of smart operators just like me. And I couldn't see any point in hanging around, wasting time.

"And then that bloody meat pie which was the ruin of me reared its ugly head.

"I really felt like feeding my face. So I bought something from these two guys, real arseholes, standing at the bus stop by an aluminium tank with steam rising from it. And these two arseholes were shouting: "Piping hot, just for you, thirty-eight kopecks for two!"

"'Are they fresh?' I asked.

"'Fresh today . . . Piping hot, just for you . . .'

"'Is there fish in them, or what?'

"'What do you mean, fish? These are real pies, meat pies. thirty-eight for two,' replied those two lying fat-guts in their dirty white coats over their sleeveless padded jackets.

"And in the twinkling of an eye I was done for. Because it was only when I had bought the two pies they were advertising and only when I was finishing off the second one, it was only then, that I realized what the fact of the matter was. And the fact of the matter was that, you see, those pies had been lying in their shop window and had dried up, and then they had steamed them thoroughly, and started flogging them out on the street to suckers like me. Of course, I immediately felt sick. But I didn't lose my head, because there's more than one way to skin a cat. So, bang! Out comes a half-bottle from my briefcase (I always take a half-bottle with me wherever I go), I sprinkle some salt in the top, let it dissolve and, to reduce any heartburn, I go and drink it all down in one, straight out of the bottle. I don't remember, but I think I was in some sort of snack bar.

"Well now, you know now, to be honest, I really don't know, how I could be to blame? After all, that's what my old dad always used to do. He had two cures when someone was ill. For a cold – vodka mixed with pepper, or if it was your stomach – vodka mixed with salt. And he would have probably lived for many a year, if it wasn't for the sodding Germans again, who killed him in the war.

"So how could I be to blame then? By saying that I was in a state of alcoholic intoxication. And those rats who probably phoned up my work and told them that I was in a state of alcoholic intoxication, those rats were all telling a pack of lies, saying that I was in a state of alcoholic intoxication. Because when I was with them I wasn't yet in a state of alcoholic intoxication. But later on, when I rang them up when I was in a state of alcoholic intoxication, they couldn't see down the telephone wires whether I was in a state of alcoholic intoxication or not in a state of alcoholic intoxication. And what they said about my speech being slurred, they were telling a pack of lies about that as well, just out of spite. My speech wasn't slurred at all, they were just offended because I'm cleverer than them and just sort of tricked them – so they decided to get their own back on me. Oh, I landed right in it!

"And this is how I landed right in it. Sure enough – as soon as I drank the vodka, my heartburn stopped right away. But, to tell you the honest truth, I badly wanted to go to the toilet.

"By now it had got dark. I took an instant dislike to this toilet I went to by the station, because it was a real piss hole. Because by now it was dark in there, it had already got dark, and there was no light in there. And guys kept coming in and you could hear them cracking all sorts of dirty jokes, which I am not prepared to repeat. I sat down in there squeamishly and did some hard thinking.

"I fell to thinking – how strange life is, how strange all her ups and downs are. For instance, what was I this morning? A candidate for the chop. And what was I now? A wise worker, brilliantly completing a responsible assignment concerning production, despite all the difficulties.

"Now, maybe it was because of the vodka, or maybe it was just forebodings, but I suddenly felt very scared. Because the water was gurgling away there, roaring underneath me. And I felt scared, first of all, since the water was roaring away, but also because I could be in for one of life's downs – what if, I thought, some underwater hand suddenly grabs me from below.

"I did my little bit of business smartish – and got out fast.

"And then it hit me like a ton of bricks! What did you wipe your arse on, you silly sod?! On the contract, which you then dropped straight into that scary, gurgling water!

"So I started groaning, burst out in a fine sweat, and dashed off immediately to phone that greenhouse shithouse out-of-town market gardeners. And they told me that I was drunk, that I had tricked the comrade manager into signing the piece of paper, which he had done, not being in complete possession of all the facts. And again, they said that I was inebriated, and so they'd been in touch with our beloved authorities and I was going to have the book thrown at me, seeing as they had the signatures of two witnesses.

"'From Norilsk, are they, those thieving witnesses of yours,' I snarled and slammed down the receiver, but not before calling them all the names under the sun, not having at my disposal any other weapon with which to combat life's grim abominations.

"Well, what happened next? What next? The next thing was – what did I have to lose?

"The poison from the meat pie was still eating away at me – so I had some more vodka and salt. To cut a long story short, I fell down in the street, but, thank God, I wasn't taken to a sobering up station, but to 'casualty'. And there Dr Tsarkov-Kolomensky, word of honour, I can't tell a lie, could scarcely stand up straight himself, he was a fat guy with a beard, looked just like a cat, boomed: "How can your family put up with you! Families fall apart because of people like you!"

"'Oh, you pig! You're a piss head yourself, and how!' I said, and unable to hold it any longer, threw up. And so they threw the book at me as well. And these days I just do my own thing. Win a few, lose a few. So there you are then, son!"

The speaker opened his eyes, which had been closed out of excitement at the very beginning of his story, and discovered that the waiting room was almost empty. The women with their bags had disappeared, as had the girls with their suitcases, the guys with their women, and the citizen with the newspaper had gone away, and only the tattooed youth was there, sleeping sweetly, resting his shaggy head on his round fist.

"Oy, buddy!" said the story teller, shaking him.

"Get up! Get up!"

A stern-looking cleaning woman arrived.

"What's all the row about, you bums!" she shouted, proudly leaning on her long mop.

"We . . . we weren't doing anything," said the guy timidly. "We're just waiting for the train. Out to Kubekovaya."

"Out to Ku-bekovaya!" said the cleaning woman with a sardonic grin. "Your train to Kubekovaya went ages ago. You'll have to move, I'm cleaning in here."

"But couldn't we," said the guy still more timidly, "wait for the next one, missus?"

"Well, mister, the next one," said the woman caustically, "is tomorrow morning, that's your next train to Kubekovaya."

"Oh well, can't be helped, we'll just have to wait till morning," suggested the guy.

"Ever seen this before?" she said.

And the woman stuck two fingers up at the guy. The guitarist woke up.

"What's all the noise about?" he barked. "We've really had enough of you, woman! I'll punch your head in!"

"I'll, I'll call the police," squealed the elderly woman, retreating.

"Oh, don't do that, don't call the police!" yelled the guy, as if wounded.

"That's right, mate," agreed the youth condescendingly. "We don't need the police. Let's get out of here, mate."

"Where to?"

"To anywhere. Let's go anywhere."

"But all the same, where to?"

"Oh . . . let's go, let's sing a song . . . 'Why you're always broke'."

"Okay, let's go," said the guy.

And off they went.

# The Circumstances Surrounding the Death of Andrei Stepanovich

I am going to tell you about how our bursar, the man in charge of the stores, died.

It happened just when we were doing our field work, while he was carrying out his official duties, head flat on the table along with the weights off the scales and the warehouse book containing notes of who'd had what on tick, in the storeroom, which had been built out of deciduous trees by the dropout Paramot. This Paramot, or Promot, was well known to everyone on the expedition – he was all mouth and trousers, there was nothing else to be said. In the season he would earn anywhere between one thousand two hundred and one thousand five hundred new roubles, and then he'd blow the lot in a week, mainly on account of his wanting to treat every Tom, Dick and Harry that he met, and travelling around in three taxis at once – the first one for his cap, the second for his sleeveless coat, and the third for the conveyance of Paramot himself – blue-eyed, fair-haired, and, as they say, with the signs of every vice etched on his face.

Yes, yes, he was a blue-eyed youth, fair-haired, and with the signs of every vice etched on his face, all of which allowed him to pass himself off as the great-nephew of Sergei Esenin, the poet.

Now last year, in the autumn, Paramot flew from Yakutia to Moscow on an Ilyushin 18 just to have a wash in the Sandunovsky baths. He took two of his friends along, both dropouts, the shot-firer Akhmetdyanov and someone who was no more than a kid, also a dropout, called Volodya Puchko, who according to his passport was seventeen years old, but to judge by his mug, was at least twenty-five.

The friends boarded the fleet-winged airliner, which bore them posthaste straight to the Sandunovsky baths, but en route they encountered the Uzbekistan restaurant, where, seating themselves on squat little pouffes, they whiled away the day, the evening, and a tiny little bit of the night, after which they found themselves in Dorogomilovo in the abode of some tender loving Muscovite tarts, where they spent the remainder of the night – they drank, savoured the bodies of the Muscovite tarts and fell sound asleep, only to wake up the next morning in a strange house, in a strange street, and naturally without a penny piece in their pockets.

They then set off for Yaroslavsky Station, refreshed themselves from their drinking bout with water from a fountain in the form of an artificial spring, climbed into a goods car where there was a little bit of coal. And the friends set off back to those parts where there were no problems over residence permission. Akhmetdyanov and Volodya were in a foul temper – spitting out curses at Moscow's soul, but Paramot was afraid of nothing and smiled – he was awfully pleased that his girl had been called Rimma. He'd wanted a girl like that for years. He'd even made up a new refrain to a song he had known since childhood:

*Steeply rises Ascension Bridge,*
*Behind the house is a mountain ridge.*
*That block is Number Thirty-Four.*
*No trendies there,*
*Only villains on every stair,*
*And forty to a flat on every floor.*

Chorus: *Rimma!!! Beauty! Argentina!*

These words, pretty pathetic, but sweet, beautiful and magical, he pronounced with gusto, making a fist with his right hand to help things along, and that was as it should be, because throughout his life Paramot always did things with gusto and impetuously, his favourite phrase went like this: "What's the difference! It's in the past! Fir-rst rate!"

Well now, the dear departed – Andrei Stepanovich, the bursar – was reckoned to be his bosom pal, but this did not correspond to the facts of the situation at all, because when they met it was only as good acquaintances and fellow-drinkers, nothing more, there was nothing heartfelt between them at all. Be that as it may, Paramot was very distressed at the bursar's sudden death and this distress was laced to a certain degree with guilty feelings on account of Botka the dog, which had caused a row between Paramot and the bursar the day before the regrettable fatality. By the end of the summer the dog Botka had become extraordinarily good looking, though his mother – the bitch Taiga – had rejected her pup soon after his birth, and all because she had been given two Eskimo pups to suckle, and since she was an Eskimo herself, she loved them more than Botka, who was the son of a mongrel and was only half-related to Eskimos.

Early that morning Andrei Stepanovich had drunk a bottle of Moskovskaya vodka and was now standing near his storehouse, his eyes fixed patiently on the sky, while the assistant drilling foreman from the ZIF–600 rig, Kolya Kharlampiev, was supposed to throw his cap right up into the sky there, so that Andrei Stepanovich might demonstrate the reliability of his hand and the accuracy of his eye. The bet was simple: he had to get four shotgun pellets in the cap or if not, the bursar was to give Kolya a litre of vodka.

The shot rang out, and Kharlampiev didn't get his vodka. And just then Paramot showed up – straight from work, from the ditches he was blasting and clearing about five kilometres from the camp, not far – along he came, and at his heels was the aforementioned Botka, the son of a bitch.

"Watch out!" shouted Paramot, and promptly explained: "I'm only joking, actually it's 'all clear' mates, what's the difference!"

And Paramot was on the point of telling some cock and bull story about trying to blow up a bear with an ammonal charge, but the bear almost blew Paramot up instead, guts and appendix the lot, when the bursar came over and said that he had taken a real shine to the dog.

"And if you give Botka to me as an act of friendship, I'll make a first-rate hunter out of him."

"No way. Ah-ha. No way," replied Paramot indifferently. I've fattened up Botka with my own hands on stewed meat, and I'm going to make rissoles and soup out of him just for myself, because I've set my heart and soul on a bit of fresh meat."

"Well, you can have a bit of beef – I've got some beef in the store, you just go and chop yourself off a decent chunk."

"Your beef's blue, Andrei Stepanovich, and it's not because you paint it, it's just naturally blue, so you can stuff yourself with it and get ill, and just forget about Botka. I'm the one who's going to eat him, not you. That's all there is to it. Finished. No way, not another peep out of you. What's the difference – it's in the past. First rate."

The bursar really took offence at Paramot, and Paramot was now afraid that the bursar had taken this offence with him to the grave. That was why Paramot was beside himself to be nice to Andrei Stepanovich, or at least to his dead body.

Paramot first noticed Andrei Stepanovich when the latter, burdened with all the cares of the world, had lain his head on the warehouse notebook to sleep the eternal sleep. Paramot could see that the storehouse door was open, that it was dark inside, because it was white as white all around on account of the snowfall the previous day.

So Paramot went into the store, where the bursar was sleeping his eternal sleep over the warehouse notebook, and it was evident that it was an eternal sleep and not just a drunken stupor, seeing as the bursar's eyes had taken on a glassy stare, were grey and bulging, and his face had gone whitish-yellow.

And right at the back of the storehouse, in the half light, all manner of comestibles were to be seen – cases of stewed meat, sugar, flour, salt, vinegar, pepper, chocolate, and the only thing Paramot couldn't see was vodka – Andrei Stepanovich had hidden it with such skill and secrecy, that he often had trouble finding it again himself.

Paramot suddenly got scared.

Not of the dead man, but scared that he, being somewhere where he shouldn't be and at a time when he shouldn't be, could be put on trial for strangling someone to get at the vodka or for some other reason.

"And then you'll get sentenced to hard labour for thousands of years for doing sweet F.A., just like Karla."

Then he went away and came into my tent, and asked me if I had any eau-de-Cologne because he wanted a drink, but I didn't have any eau-de-Cologne for him, and then Paramot let it drop to me that our bursar was dead, and one look at his face told me it was true, and I went off to get some eau-de-Cologne from Lida from Irkutsk, the goods train worker, and she gave me some, only it wasn't eau-de-Cologne, it was Lights of Moscow perfume. . . I gave the Lights to Paramot, who was shaken to the core.

And I myself went over to the storehouse, where that peculiar hubbub had already begun – the fuss and bother, negotiations, weeping and then more fuss and bother, which always accompany funerals, weddings and births – those manifestations of life, beginnings, middles and ends.

Then the corpse had to be transported back to base, to which end we called out Stepan, the driver of a GAZ–51, called him up and told him to bring a case of Moskovskaya with him for the wake "in the field".

The Lights of Moscow perfume hadn't had the slightest effect on Paramot and hadn't even made him pensive, so with unusual agility he set about knocking together a coffin out of some sawn-up planks, never for a moment entertaining the thought that they would transport his friend on the truck without his being properly packaged, like a side of meat or something.

Now Olga Ivanovna, the cook, the one who at that time had had her head shaved and been deported from Yakutia for dissolute behaviour, though where to was unknown, she baked three great piles of pancakes, and made a bucket of blancmange out of condensed milk.

And we raised our cups in honour of the bursar Andrei Stepanovich Golikov, a man who in no way, no way at all, stood out from the other people around him: he told lies, he always had his petty vanities, he had ended up in Yakutia donkey's years ago for telling jokes, and after he was rehabilitated, he got used to the life there, he managed various little shops, had his hand in the till from time to time, liked a drop to drink, short-changed each of us of the odd rouble note, not to say of the odd ten roubles – this very ordinary man now lay there in a rough and ready coffin, which Paramot, an inveterate dropout, had knocked together for him, he lay there in the coffin under the branches of the fir trees, totally impassive.

I have already said that there had been a snowfall, but when the lid was being nailed on the coffin, you could hardly see anything ten metres away, because a fresh helping of snow descended from the sky, covered everything, and started swirling up, large fluffy flakes, and small hard ones – all mixed up together and falling to the ground at an angle.

Stepan was at the wheel – an unhurried, sluggish man, and Paramot sat beside him, like an escort – that was the role he played, and Andrei Stepanovich was in the back – safely ensconced in his cask.

The engine roared into life, banged, belched, and the yellow, horizontal pools of light from the headlights absorbed the snowflakes and slowly moved off parallel to the ground.

So there you have it. The mountains are steep in Yakutia. There is a permanent wind blowing down off them. The party was on its way. Paramot, in floods of tears, was telling the indifferent Stepan about Andrei Stepanovich's good qualities.

"I see," responded Styopa gloomily, a man who couldn't care less, who didn't give a damn, a man you could never surprise, who knew and understood everything that went on around him and who didn't want to play the least part in it, not even in his thoughts. But Paramot – he was a different case, but now I'm repeating myself, after all, you know him well enough already.

Now on the way there was a fairly steep incline and the truck could scarcely make it. It felt as though it wasn't moving at all, just stuck on the spot – that's how steep the incline was.

So at the top they switched off the engine, drank a drop of vodka, and had a look, and found that the coffin had vanished, perhaps it had slipped out because of the steepness of the incline.

So, cursing and swearing, they walked back down through the snowstorm and found the coffin in the midst of the blizzards right on the other side of a brook.

So they pushed it back up the hill, the coffin that is, worked up a sweat, and when they had slung it on the back of the truck, Paramot started to look at it, and the yellow moon was reflected in his eyes, waxing, growing bigger, larger.

"Hey, Styopa, this coffin here, it, hm, don't look like it's ours," said Paramot, horror-struck.

Styopa spat and pulled Paramot into the cab, and Paramot tried to break free, started tearing at his collar, and yelling wildly in the light of the moon, which illuminated the ugly white ground.

And it seemed that you could hear in the snowstorm, squeaking and rattling, that huge and lifeless mechanism which makes the Earth go round: "Scra-ape, cre-ak, clunk-clunk-clunk, scra-ape, cre-ak, clunk-clunk-clunk. . ."

# The Portrait of F. L. Jailbreaker, Esq.

One summer a visitor from Moscow was journeying through the wide open spaces of Siberia. The visitor from Moscow was astonished by everything he saw and it was all to his liking: state of the art buildings soaring up to the sky, ribbons of rivers and roads, the faces of the people and their jaws champing on Siberian pine sap. The visitor from Moscow was touched by much that he saw: the girl leaning her head on the shoulder of her sweetheart, his army field shirt thick with grime, lads who had drawn pictures of Paul McCartney and The Rolling Stones on their T-shirts, the bright eyes of Siberian old men and women. The man from Moscow knew life.

And so it was that on one occasion he popped into the collective farm market of a small regional Siberian town. The Muscovite loved markets, the hustle and the bustle, the merriment, a Georgian tossing a water melon in the air, an Uzbek calling on Allah as his witness, and the Russian peasant quietly standing in a queue for beer.

The traveller checked out the prices of the fruit and vegetables. He noted: pine strawberries at 3 roubles 50 kopecks, cucumbers at 2 roubles 30 kopecks, onions at 1 rouble 50 kopecks. And there too in the market he saw the portrait of F. L. Jailbreaker, Esq.

Right there in the market, hanging on a wall, in a glass case, were some photographs, all unified by an eye-catching caption which read: THESE PEOPLE ARE PREVENTING US FROM LIVING.

The visitor took a keen interest in this and was fully rewarded for doing so with the series of unsavoury mugshots that stared out at him – most of them with swollen, vacant eyes. But F. L. Jailbreaker clearly stood apart from the others.

F. L. Jailbreaker stood apart from the others by virtue of his unusually clear gaze and his bright and breezy manner. Because all the other inhabitants of the photo display case stood hunched up, stood there with their hands outstretched in supplication towards the camera lens.

But F. L. Jailbreaker beheld the world in a somewhat impudent fashion, he had a freshly trimmed curly beard, and his large torso was clad in a sailor's striped vest, and over the vest F. L. Jailbreaker wore a jacket. There you have it!

And the words underneath F. L. Jailbreaker which explained in full his situation were as follows: F. L. JAILBREAKER ESQ., BORN 1939, HAS, SINCE JANUARY 1973, NOT HAD A JOB ANYWHERE, GETS DRUNK ALL THE TIME AND LEADS A PARASITIC, ANTISOCIAL LIFE.

The visitor from Moscow fell deep in thought.

Now nearby there happened to be two policemen, their grey shirts worn outside their trousers. They were altogether absorbed in their own conversation, while supervising the trading going on around and occasionally fingering the leather gun holsters that protruded from their shirts.

Overcoming his innate reserve, the Muscovite visitor politely addressed the custodians of law and order: "Comrades, if this object falls under your jurisdiction, please allow me to take off your hands once and for all the portrait of F. L. Jailbreaker."

The policemen were quite taken aback.

"It does, it does," they replied eventually, seeing that there stood before them a respectable-looking man with a briefcase. "Only what do you want it for?"

"Well, you know, let me just try and explain to you," said the visitor from Moscow. "Despite the fact that Citizen Jailbreaker is obviously a thoroughly negative type, he does exude a sort of inner strength, there is somehow sort of something in his appearance, which to a large extent inspires confidence. He invigorates one."

The policemen perked up.

"Yes, eh well," said one of them in agreement – the skinny, pale one. "He's a past master at inspiring confidence. Once he gets going, you'll be all ears! He'll go on nineteen to the dozen about the devil knows what. He goes on about God and Jesus Christ in particular. Yet he's a Molokan or something, isn't he? He goes on about religion all the time. Isn't that right, Ryabov?" he said, turning to the other policeman.

"Ah-ha. Dead right, Grisha," nodded the blue-eyed, elderly Ryabov. "He's done his studying. But he's not a Molokan, because," at this point the policeman paused significantly, "because he's a Jew by religion."

Having said this, Ryabov took off his uniform cap and wiped the inside of it with a handkerchief, and repeated: "He's a Jew by religion, born in Krepovka."

"Ah well now, Krepovka is it." said Grisha, bestirring himself. "If he's from Krepovka, then he's a Molokan. The Molokans live in Krepovka."

"That's not where the Molokans live at all, that's where the Jews live," said Ryabov, putting on his cap. "They were exiled there under the tsar. They're all Russians to look at, but their faith is Jewish. They were exiled, and they petitioned the tsar to give their settlement a name. And so the tsar gave them a name – the village of Judino. It was only after Lenin came along that it was renamed Krepovka."

"Excuse me," interrupted the traveller, "Was that in honour of that peasant called Krepov who corresponded with Lev Tolstoy? And Lev Tolstoy called him his brother. And he also wrote some book or other, that Krepov. About agriculture and sponging off others. I read in the *Literary Gazette* . . ."

"That's right," said Ryabov. "I come from these parts myself. That's dead right that it got its name from some peasant or other. And seeing as it's called Krepovka, then it must have been named after Krepov."

"Then how come Lev Nikolaevich Tolstoy would start corresponding with some Jew?" asked Grisha malevolently. "I'm telling you, half the village there are Jews, and half are Molokans. And then, if he was a Jew, then he wouldn't go on about Christ. Because Jews don't believe in Christ, they only believe in Saturday. You've got sod all chance of getting them to do a day's work on a Saturday. That's for sure."

"And are you saying then that Molokans believe in Christ? Go and look in their houses – you won't find a single icon there."

"So what, if there aren't any icons there," retorted his opponent. It's true Molokans don't have any icons, but they still believe in Christ. And Jailbreaker there says that Christ was a socialist, and that it was Cain who fathered all the bastards in the world, but he himself was born of Abel."

"Oh get lost! Molokans, sons of Abel. You haven't got a clue what you're talking about!" Ryabov turned away with a wave of his hand.

"Oh, now don't you think this is going a bit too far?" said the Muscovite, wading into the conversation again, pointing at the display case. "I mean, what you have written here – that he's leading a parasitic life, getting drunk all the time?"

"No," answered the policemen bitterly. "It's the stark naked truth. He's never had a job anywhere, he drinks like a fish, and fools give him money."

"And yet it *so happens* that he hasn't worked since January 1973," said the visitor, not giving up. "Perhaps the man hasn't yet been able to find anything suitable in the town. It's only six months altogether, after all."

"Oh, come on," sniggered the policeman by the name of Grisha ironically. "Last year he only worked two days altogether. When they brought him into the station the first time, I asked him: 'Surname, first name, patronymic,' and he says: 'Razin, Stepan, Timofeevich.' And he's grinning all over his face, bold as brass!"

"He's no Molokan or Jew," said the policeman called Ryabov, suddenly losing his temper. "He's a full-blown dropout – only he pulls the wool over everyone's eyes. Would a Molokan or Jew guzzle so much vodka? He can put down half a litre in the time it takes three of us to get through a quarter. I've seen it myself – a citizen bought a half litre of Extra vodka in the Food Store, and our man there dashed into the shop. 'Could I just have a look.'

Snatches the bottle out of the citizen's hands, bites the top off and pours the whole lot down his filthy fat gob. Downed it in one and then he was off. It was mind-blowing."

The policeman spat.

"What do you mean, downed it in one?" gasped the visitor from Moscow.

"Just that – he just went and downed it," explained Ryabov. "Opened his trap wide, poured it in, spat out the bits of glass and walked off."

"Well, anyway, he's no Jew," said Grisha. "Maybe he's not a Molokan either, but he's no Jew. . ."

And who knows where this lengthy argument regarding F. L. Jailbreaker's religious denomination would have finished, if suddenly a commotion hadn't run through the bazaar.

The policemen pulled themselves up and started acting stern. A tall guy with a smirk on his face was making his way through the rows of tradesmen's stalls. He was waving his arms about and shouting something. Old women bowed to the guy respectfully. The guy grabbed a cucumber and stuffed it in his beard. When he reached the display case all that could be heard was a munching sound issuing from the deeper recesses of his peasant beard. And you didn't have to be a Muscovite to recognize the new arrival as F. L. Jailbreaker.

F. L. Jailbreaker looked attentively at his likeness.

"Still there then?" he asked sharply.

"Still there," replied the policemen curtly. "And have you found yourself a job yet, Falen Lukich?"

"I've already told you!" said Jailbreaker, eagle-eyed. "Unless they offer me a basic wage of two hundred and fifty roubles a month as befits my intellectual ability, I'm not going to find a job."

"Come on, our boss only gets a hundred and fifty," said the policemen, unable to contain themselves. "And look what you're after, you cheeky so-and-so!"

"That just goes to show that his brains are only worth a hundred and fifty roubles. All I need is what is essential to keep body and soul together," said Jailbreaker, pointing to his body, which required the two hundred and fifty roubles.

"Just you cut out the jokes about Tishchenko," responded the policemen, rudely interrupting him. "This is your last chance – we're giving you three days, and then you'll be sorry."

"What are you shouting for all of a sudden," said Jailbreaker in conciliatory tones. "You mustn't shout at people. Christ ordered us not to shout at anyone. Ah, if Christ were alive today – he'd slip me two hundred and fifty a month. He wouldn't begrudge me. And you, respected citizens, not to say comrades, by the way, please oblige a fellow with a smoke. Please let me have something to have a quick drag on."

The policemen hesitated, and the visitor from Moscow also wanted to take part in the proceedings.

"Perhaps you'd like to smoke one of mine? They're American. Winstons. Have you ever tried them?"

"I can smoke American cigarettes as well," agreed Jailbreaker. "In the light of the international situation, I can smoke American. Give us a couple, mate, if you don't mind."

And he snatched a handful from the Moscow visitor's shiny packet. He tucked them behind his ears and shoved them into the thick undergrowth of his beard.

"What a funny surname you've got!" said the visitor from Moscow jocularly, giving Jailbreaker a light from his gas lighter. Some parents you must have had, eh? Leaving you a name like that!"

At this F. L. Jailbreaker, in full view of all those present, went completely berserk. His hair stood on end, his eyes went bloodshot, and the cigarette sticking out of his mouth looked like a cossack lance.

"What did you say about my parents, you fat-gobbed shithead?!" said Jailbraker with a hefty intake of breath, and he stretched out his hand to seize the visitor from Moscow by the lapels.

"Now, now, keep your hands to yourself, Jailbreaker!" shouted the policemen, interposing themselves between him and the visitor from Moscow for the latter's protection.

"Oh, no. He wasn't going to do anything," said the visitor, backing off. "Beneath that rough exterior there lurks a heart of gold. Please don't take offence, comrade Jailbraker. I didn't mean anything."

"Then don't shoot your mouth off for nothing, if you didn't mean it," concluded Jailbreaker with pleasure, blew out some smoke with relish and remained living in Siberia for ever more.

The visitor from Moscow hastened back to Moscow. There he now works, as he did before, at a publishers whose name begins with M. The management is very pleased with him, and he was due to get a good bonus, come the holiday. But his wife took practically all of it away from him, because she wanted to buy herself a mink coat. She had seen lots of different films at private showings, and so she wanted a mink coat. And you know, a thing like that costs a huge sum of money. So there is a typical example for you of the negative influence of bourgeois aesthetics on a weak soul.

# The Train from Kazan

Once, while travelling on a trolley bus, a certain citizen was collecting in the money from the people, so as to pay for them all, handing over the money to the driver and receiving tickets for the money he handed over. He was doing this because the ticket machine, a newfangled automatic one, in which you put your money, pull the handle and receive a torn off ticket to show the inspector, was not working. When he had collected in the money, the citizen was confronted with general confusion, for he did not know who had handed over money and how much he had passed on, and a lot of the people had got mixed up and shouts could be heard: "Who's paid? I didn't pay fifteen kopecks. I paid for two and I want six kopecks change. No, that's not right – you owe them money, and I've got to have three kopecks off of them to give to them . . ."

"Ah-ha, I see. Fiddling," said the citizen dejectedly, and left the trolley bus while it was still moving.

The noise immediately abated and the trolley bus stopped.

And the strapping great driver, without a word, without even looking at the passengers, came out of the cabin specially constructed separately for him, made his way to the rear door, and there addressed the spotty young man, who was timidly clutching at the nickel-plated handle: "You were the one who helped him open the folding doors, so you can go after him."

And he pushed the young man out of the vehicle, but while he was returning to his cabin to sit at the wheel again and continue the journey, as far as the terminus, as far as the railway station, they both – the one who'd been fiddling and the youth – boarded the bus once again before the doors had had time to close, and they quietly stood in the corner.

"It's a disgrace! It's a downright disgrace! When's this universal disgrace ever going to end! After all, they're all collectively guilty, the citizen who was fiddling, that uncouth driver, the young man, and all the others who kept quiet, and especially the ticket machine!!" I said to myself indignantly.

Okay then. The trolley bus eventually got to the station, I got off the trolley bus and went to the information bureau to find out – well, when finally the train from Kazan would arrive.

There behind a glass partition, at a desk by a telephone, sat a not altogether young woman, and she was saying something into the receiver which I couldn't hear at all through the glass.

You see, she was talking and talking on the phone. Who to? I wanted to ask her through the glass when finally the train from Kazan would be coming. I needed to know when the train from Kazan was coming, and she was just talking away on the phone. What about? I waited. The queue of people waited. They were all waiting. They started shouting. I kept quiet. I have my pride.

"Miss, is this an information bureau or what?" enquired a native Siberian in a sheepskin coat loudly, audaciously pushing his way to the front.

"Yes, it is, it is," replied the people in the queue amicably.

"I know it is," explained the loud-mouthed Siberian, "I know that all right, but what about her there, does she?!"

And he pointed a brown finger at the female clerk, who paid not the slightest attention, and who was talking blithely and obliviously into the phone.

"Let's go and see the station manager right now," someone threatened. "Let him tell us straight whether the railway information bureau is open or not."

Fat lot of difference that made – she still carried on talking on the phone nineteen to the dozen, without batting an eyelid, always on the phone, on the phone, forever on the the phone, the phone . . .

"Well, yer won't get 'old of the manager," explained a shaven-headed youngster with a cheerful grin. "His office ain't open from twelve to two."

"What a disgrace! An absolute downright disgrace! This is terrible. The absolute inertia of a duty clerk, the complacent and somewhat cynical remarks of people in the queue. I'm downright worn out," I said to myself again indignantly.

I knew that I would leave the queue any minute now, without even waiting for any information about the train from Kazan.

I knew that I would read on a wall some advert like:

FLORENA
FACIAL CREAM FROM GERMANY
KEEPS YOUR SKIN FRESH
BUY FLORENA

"Right then, I'll buy myself some of that wonderful cream," I'll say to myself, "After all, it smells fresh."

I'll go up to a little drug and perfume stall and say. I'll say "Wowee" because the stall will be open, but there won't be any salesgirl there. There will be some Florena cream from Germany there, Matador eau-de-Cologne, Troinoi eau-de-Cologne, Neva razor blades, Baltika razor blades, Caesar razor blades, toothbrushes, powders, medicines, drugs, pomades, perfumes, playing cards, handkerchiefs, and more Florena cream from Germany, but there just won't be any salesgirl, any salesgirl at all at the stall.

"What a disgrace! Feckless carryings on! An absolute disgrace! Terrible behaviour! Universal terrible behaviour! Fecklessness, carelessness, negligence and loutishness!" I'll shout to myself.

Incidentally, I'll then walk all over town for hours discovering disorderliness and disgraces. Either I'll get water poured over my head from an open window, or maybe it'll be tea, or the traffic lights at the crossroads will break down, or some little boys, still only children, will be playing some game on a park bench, and when I tell them off, they'll tell me to go f— my mother.

Afterwards I will observe that evening is approaching, and it has come about that my working day is also at an end. I will go home. There, sternly but at the same time lovingly, I will cast an eye on my kith and kin, eat some soup and sit down to read some entertaining book or other, a novel of some sort, for example . . . I don't know what for example . . .

And if you ask me, if you shout to yourself: "And who do you think you are then" then I'll be happy to tell you a little about myself.

I am thirty-two years old. I am a white collar worker myself. I do not have a higher education, but I have been working for a long time, in a laboratory, I'm only thirty-two years of age but I'm already almost completely bald. Non-Party member. I love my work, but not very much. I don't love women, but sometimes I do. At the present moment I am acting head of the laboratory. My boss has gone off on a business trip to Bugulma. He is returning via Kazan. I'm bored. I really like everything to be in order and as it should be. I walk all over town all day, out of boredom making sure that everything is in order. I understand perfectly well that in my own case not all is as it should be – now what's this – walking around town and poking my nose into other people's business during working hours. "This really is a disgrace! This really won't do! Awful!" I sometimes whisper to myself.

And then I get to thinking that I'm the one who is the biggest good-for-nothing and scoundrel of all.

# Quiet Evlampiev and Homo Futurum

Now this is what happened to the quiet engineer Evlampiev, when on one nice balmy July evening he came out onto the asphalt path in front of his stone-built block of flats to take a breath of the fresh cool air, illuminated as it was by the unearthly radiance of the distant moon, to discard the tension of his day at work, which had been spent cursing and swearing at some high-handed rep of one of the firm's customers, to ready himself for the magical July night to be spent with his young wife Zina, a draughtswoman, who at that very moment, having made up the bed, was laying out cards on the white tablecloth for a game of patience, having tenderly told Evlampiev by way of farewell: "Now, Grishenka, mind you don't go far, or I'll start getting worried about you . . ."

Evlampiev smiled at the simplicity and tenderness of his partner, and he was turning over in his mind various smart answers he could make to some of the impertinent comments that that vulgar Pigarev had made, when he was suddenly stopped by a voice, soft and consonant with the weather.

"Fancy a beer, comrade?"

Evlampiev shuddered, though altogether pointlessly: before him stood an extraordinarily peaceable fellow in a gabardine mackintosh, and he was also smiling at Evlampiev – the good-natured smile of an elderly mouth.

"Well, actually, it's too late," answered Evlampiev, straightening his spectacles and indicating the open-air beer stall with which he was familiar and which had been a hive of activity during the heat of the day.

"Oh, come now!" said the mackintosh, his smile yawning ever

wider. "For a good man. . . look, I've got a bit . . . I got three litres this afternoon, what do I need all that for?"

And he led Evlampiev off to the moonlit shadows of the beer stall and quickly pulled out of the weeds there a jar that had already been opened of that drink which ordinary folk find so congenial.

"Oh no, no I can't, it's late," protested Evlampiev weakly.

But he soon gave in, subdued by the unintrusive politeness of his companion and the harmonious glint of the clean glass tumbler, the very sight of which negated any hasty thought there may have been regarding the unhygienic infection being offered.

"You just give me one rouble thirty-eight kopecks for all this. The cost price was eighty-eight kopecks, then fifty kopecks for my trouble, I don't need a lot," the host's voice kept babbling away.

"Yes, of course. There's one rouble fifty, take that, of course," said Evlampiev, still embarrassed for some unknown reason.

"And there's twelve kopecks' change," replied the beer-supplier kindly.

"There's no need for that!" said Evlampiev with a wave of his hand.

"Oh, yes there is," said the man in the mackintosh and he suddenly became sterner and even, as so often happens, grew in stature. "I don't need what doesn't belong to me, otherwise you can give me my beer back. I'm not some sort of speculator!"

Knocked completely off his stroke, Evlampiev put the change in his jacket pocket and, timidity itself, offered to share the evening's feast with the punctilious stranger.

"Now that's a different matter," the latter agreed graciously, and knocked back two or three glasses on the trot without turning a hair. Evlampiev had a drink too.

"Now, of course, you're anxious to find out who I am," said the stranger suddenly. "Now don't deny it, young man, I can see this question in your sincere eyes. But first of all I. . . Now let me get you right first. So . . . Of course, you've got a higher education and you probably earn unheard of heaps of money."

"There's nothing unheard of about it," said the slightly inebriated Evlampiev with a smile. "A hundred and twenty roubles and then sometimes there's a quarterly bonus. "

"Jesus Christ! That's terrible! You're a millionaire!" said the stranger, rocking from side to side. "And what do you do, you madman, with a heap of money like that?"

"What do you mean?" said Evlampiev, taken aback. "I spend it. I'm a married man, by the way," he added for some reason.

"That's understood," agreed the stranger, likewise for some unknown reason. "But your wife probably earns something similar to you. These stacks of cash – what do you need them for?"

"What do you mean, what do I need them for?" said Evlampiev, feeling some irritation. "Eating, drinking, buying books . . . I can't itemize the whole lot, can I? I still haven't paid off the loan from my wedding."

"That's just it, said the stranger sadly, "With such huge sums of money as that, it's inevitable that you get just as much unheard of expense too."

"Well, what about you?" said Evlampiev angrily.

"Me?" smiled the stranger enigmatically.

"Yes! You! What about you? What are you then?"

"I'll tell you 'what about me' and 'what I am then', only you won't believe a word of it. I'll tell you, and you won't believe me at all, because I live without any money at all."

"What, you mean, without any at all, at all?" said Evlampiev ironically.

"At all, at all. And I can see by your smile that you're suspicious of me, so I'll answer you straight that I live without any money at all, and I even live a proper, clean and good life."

"I'd like to know how?" said Evlampiev, still trying to be witty.

"Well, now you're going to find out. Well, let's start with the most important thing, your daily bread, as they say. When you want to get hold of it, you pop into the Comfort café, for example. There you eat some dried up broiled chicken – and that gives you ulcers. But I don't. Very qui-ietly I take my favourite table by the window in the health canteen, and there I get given straight off a drop of vegetable soup – nine kopecks a plateful, stewed cabbage, very economical, – five kopecks, a drop of tea without sugar – one kopeck, bit of bread – free. Altogether – fifteen kopecks. All nice and healthy."

"And does it fill you up?"

"Yes it does. And I won't get ulcers."

"But it's still money, even if it were thirteen kopecks," said Evlampiev, not giving in.

"It's not even thirteen, but fifteen. "But between you and me, what's that in terms of money? It's just star dust, not money. Now let's go on. After my daily bread, I might want some spiritual nourishment. So what do I do? I go to a bookshop, for example, where some personage, wondering whether to buy or not, is ponderously leafing though some splendid reproductions of, for example, that Western artist Picasso, with the book costing a hundred and sixty roubles. So I latch onto him from behind and look at all the pictures as well, enriching my horizons. And my eye moistens, moistens, and my face glows with spiritual joy. Do you get my drift?"

"I do. I do completely," said Evlampiev. "But there's the family. Don't you have any family obligations?"

"I'm not married," said the stranger.

"Yes, but when all's said and done, what about. . . women then?" asked the demure Evlampiev, becoming too involved.

"We-ell! Now, now, now! Whatever can I say to you!" His interlocutor wagged his finger at him. "There is something immoral about this – making love, making the availability of a woman, dependent on MONEY! Do you realize what you're proclaiming?" he asked Evlampiev reproachfully.

Evlampiev was silent.

"Then let me tell you something else. Let me tell you about clothing. I have actually become convinced that, strange as it may seem, there's no need to buy clothes at all. Because these days everybody buys new clothes, and what do they do with the old ones? Put them in the second-hand shop – who'll buy them there? The flea markets have all shut down. So people give them to me. Just take a look – what about this really nicely made mackintosh, this cap I've got on, went out of fashion in 1964, and my winkle-picker shoes which nobody wears these days?"

And he started turning pirouettes in front of Evlampiev. And Evlampiev stayed silent.

"But that's not the main thing," said the whirling fraudster, bringing his intelligent face close to Evlampiev. "That's not the main thing that keeps me warm. The main thing that keeps me warm, the main thing is that I am, as it were, a prototype of the man of the future, Homo Futurum, if I can express myself so."

"If you like," said Evlampiev.

"Not 'if I like', but precisely. You know, soon the day will come when nobody will have any money. You read the newspapers and go to meetings. You can, of course, say that I'm getting things mixed up and that I'm misunderstanding the situation. And my answer to you would be that I understand the situation perfectly well and that I'm getting nothing mixed up. Well now, let's suppose that we're going to have plenty of everything. But that doesn't mean that we're all going to stuff ourselves on broilers, giving ourselves ulcers and changing velvet for brocade every day. It doesn't mean that, does it? And if it doesn't mean that, then it must mean that I am the prototype of the man of the future. Oh, how people will remember me in the future, how they'll remember me in the future! People will remember that once upon a time used to be this one oddball, who, when there was nothing but rainy days, had no money at all, just at a time when everybody else had it. Oh, how people will remember!"

And he raised his confident hands up to heaven.

And quiet Evlampiev suddenly stopped him by grabbing him sternly by the shoulder.

"And how would you like me to smash your face in?" he suddenly suggested completely naturally.

"What for? For my kindness?" said the stranger, taking offence.

"No, not for your kindness, but for a rouble. Let me give you a rouble, and I'll punch you in the mug for it. Do you want me to?"

"No, I don't," answered the stranger, after giving it some thought.

"Well, why not?" smirked Evlampiev bloodthirstily.

"Well, because it won't do anyone any good. Neither you, nor me. You'll be spending your rouble on an anti-humane act. And, as I can see in you a man who has read the works of Fyodor Mikhailovich Dostoevsky, I am in no doubt at all that you would suffer terribly afterwards and would come grovelling to me with your kisses. It's no good for someone to give me a good hiding and then kiss me for one and the same rouble. Let's make it two, shall we?"

"Oh, no. Whatever are you saying. In fact, I was just . . . you know," said Evlampiev, faltering. "You just got me all mixed up with your logical paradoxes, when in actual fact . . . I feel a bit ashamed," he said with a wry smile.

"Yes, of course. Hitting a man in exchange for money in order to satisfy your own bestial whims has its attractions!" confirmed the stranger.

They fell silent.

"But do you know what?" suggested the stranger unexpectedly. "Do you know what – you make it three roubles. Maybe that will set your mind at rest."

"Are you sure?" asked Evlampiev.

"Absolutely sure," said the stranger, without batting an eyelid.

"But I haven't got that much money on me, I've got it at home, but not here," said Evlampiev.

"Well come on then, let's go back to your place, I suppose it's near here," guessed the stranger.

"Yes, it is," mumbled Evlampiev gloomily.

"So let's go then," said the stranger.

And off they went, off they went along the asphalt path to that quiet stone-built block of flats, quiet Evlampiev and Homo Futurum. Drops of dew had formed on the asphalt. The five-storeyed houses were falling asleep. And the cool of the night, as fresh as fresh could be, wafted around them, around quiet Evlampiev and Homo Futurum, the fresh cool of the night, illuminated by the unworldly radiance of the distant moon, which had seen it all before.

# The Material of the Future

You read in the newspapers and people are always saying that in manufacturing firms and other factories the incidence of theft by the workforce of goods of little value and things that wear out quickly has increased. Some woman standing in a queue said: "My Seryozha promised me. He promised me. There's some cloth for rubbing down machine components that they make at his factory. It's such brilliant stuff that you can easily make yerself a really stylish yellowy-green dress out of two bits of it. It's really beautiful. It's brilliant. He promised me."

And her companion went along with her.

"Yes," she remarked, "Yes. And my Alfred always has those thick towels coming his way, so he brings 'em home from work. We only dry ourselves on them once and then we just chuck the bloody things out."

The companion really let herself go, turned red in the face, her beautiful blonde tresses sticking out from under her fluffy Orenburg headscarf. She waved her hand clenching the chit for her sausages and added: "I hate 'em. I hate those thick towels. And it's all wrong what they say in *Health* magazine when they tell you to rub yourself with them to put the colour back in your cheeks. That's a mistake. When we've finished with them we throw them out right away. When we've finished with them Alfred uses them to clean his gun."

"Where'd he get a gun from?"

"Where from? From nowhere. Made it himself. Got a spanner, screws, bolts. Golden hands, that's what he's got, golden hands, my Alfred!"

I got awfully depressed when I heard these vile, shameless words like this. Golden hands! How the unknown wife of Alfred who filches things from work has debased this lofty concept! What's going on in this country, comrades? People always nicking stuff from work. And they talk in public about all their fiddling without even turning a hair!"

I got awfully depressed. I got so depressed that I promptly left the queue, especially as they'd run out of sausages by then anyway.

Always nicking stuff. A bit of this or that for their own personal needs. Anywhere you like – you're walking along minding your own business, and someone will pull you round a corner and say: "Psst! Keep it quiet! D'yer need a bit of this or that?"

They pull you away, pull something out of their pocket, or out of their shirtfront, or from under their cap – rubber bands, spanners, lenses, hosepipes, tubing, clothing, string, ironmongery.

It's terrible! And the main thing is, they're all so free and easy about it. What do you hear them say! We couldn't give a toss. The country won't be any the poorer for it. Who couldn't you give a toss for? For yourselves, you villains! Can't you see, you're nicking stuff from yourselves, from the people!

Just you look –

"Our neighbour, Bigmouth Vlas, pinches wire cord from the tyre factory."

Just you listen –

"Old Zhora brought home a roll of photographic paper yesterday."

It's disgraceful! Unbelievable!

Right here, for example, not long ago, some people had a wedding in their flat, and it went on for three days.

They got through untold quantities of cognac, wine, vodka, champagne and homebrew. And ate about two hundred roubles' worth of food.There were two accordionists playing, and there was the radiogram and the tape recorder going. They were dancing in the yard, and one woman even passed out down there. Right in the middle of a gipsy dance.

All the drunken guests were running around not knowing what was going on. They were just crying. The woman would have died if it hadn't been for a quick-thinking chap who happened to be passing – he was a sergeant major in the Reserve. He said, "It's nothing serious, just give me a minute," and he called an ambulance, and that's what saved the woman's life, and then they all carried on enjoying themselves.

And they were so pleased at the happy outcome of the woman collapsing that there wasn't a peep out of any of them when the sergeant major joined in the celebrations and started romping around with the rest of them as if he were a member of the family. And in fact, he made himself at home in no time at all. You could hear his booming voice all over the place: "And that's why I love you, and that's why you're human! Human, do you understand?"

They understood. They kept kissing each other, putting their arms round each other, and before they knew it the third night of the wedding had come – and at last the young couple were able to repair to their marriage bed. And the other guests to their beds. One on the bed, another under the table, someone else under a stool. One of the accordionists, for example, slept in the corner, standing up. He'd doze off for a while, then play a bit of "Farewell, Slav girls" and then go back to sleep again. Everyone was asleep.

Everyone was asleep. The flat was plunged into sleep. The only things to flutter in the thick air were spurned amorous advances, Cupids, Venuses, water nymphs, wood demons and other products of irrationalism, of mysticism and of bacchanalian vapours, hearkening with disapproval to the snores which emanated from many quarters.

They were asleep. Then suddenly something unpleasant happened to the young couple and disturbed their slumbers. And they woke up. She first, then he. They lay there, without speaking.

"Why can't you sleep?" asked the groom hoarsely.

"Just can't," answered the bride. "Don't know why."

And she sighed and scratched herself under the shoulder blade.

"Just go to sleep," advised the groom, and also scratched himself.

And suddenly they both started scratching themselves like mad, furiously.

"What is it?" asked the groom in fright. "Perhaps you've got bedbugs?"

"No, we haven't got bedbugs," the girl assured him, still scratching away.

"We sprayed everything on Friday. Used four canisters."

"Yes. It's not bedbugs. Bedbugs don't bite like this. Bedbugs really sting you. We had bedbugs in our hostel once, and then they came and sprayed them," said the groom. And then he thought about it, and said: "Maybe it is bedbugs after all? Shall we have a look?"

And they got up.

It was early morning, that time of the summer when the rays of the sun, before it has risen, don't shine directly into your living quarters, but rather fill them with their whitish, misty, their glorious, dawning glow.

And they got up and started looking at one another.

And they were good looking. Both were well-formed. They too were glorious in the glow of the sun's rays, if I may make so bold as to express it so.

Only, unfortunately, significant areas of their skin – young, smooth and phosphorescent – turned out to be covered in some sort of bumps with some sort of threads sticking to the bumps. White threads.

Discovering this dreadful fact, the groom dashed over to the bed and suddenly understood everything.

"Right," he said. "That's just beautiful."

The bride also understood everything. She burst into tears. The guests started to wake up.

"Who's the shit who made our bed up with this sheet?" enquired the groom, pulling on his trousers.

"It wasn't any shit, it was my mum. Don't you dare call her that! Don't you dare!" sobbed the bride, doing up her buttons. "Don't you dare! It was a present. It's a surprise. It's the material of the future."

"Who's the silly bitch who gave us this sodding material of the future?" he said, rounding on her.

"It wasn't a silly bitch, it was our dear old granny, who doesn't know anything about technology. She gave it to us. Don't you remember? No, you were as pissed as a pudding, you prat!"

"Me – pissed?!" asked the groom, losing his temper.

And he tried to remember, and eventually he succeeded in remembering that someone – perhaps it really was their granny – had indeed, right at the height of the wedding celebrations, brought along and given them some wonderful material – you could even call it, the material of the future. They showed the material to the guests and held it up to the light. All the guests admired it. The material was white, but was suffused with all the colours of the rainbow.

"It doesn't sink in water, and it doesn't burn in fire," said someone. Probably Granny.

Uncle Kolya spilt wine over the material, but the material didn't get stained with the wine.

Fyodor put a cigarette lighter to it, but it didn't catch fire.

The groom's mother-in-law did though: "This is the wonder material of the future. It will make wonderful sheets for everyone, but first of all for our young couple. Let's make the bed, eh?"

"Yes, let's make the bed! Let's make the bed!" roared the drunken guests. Let's make the bed. Kiss the bride! Hurray!"

So they made the bed. Kiss the bride. Hurray.

"Me – pissed? I'll show you!" said the groom, now fully dressed, shouting and swearing.

"Oy, what's all the noise for?!" shouted the bride's father cheerfully, coming in. And others came in.

"Just look," said the unhappy bride, pointing.

They all looked in the bed and saw that the sheet, the material of the future, was by now not a sheet at all, and not the material of the future, though it was something. It had completely decomposed, totally exposing its inner structure, which consisted of synthetic fibres and tiny needles, something that the man in the street couldn't fathom at all. They called Granny.

"Where did you get hold of all this, you old crow?"

Granny answered cautiously: "A nice man on the corner by the grocer's shop sold it to me."

"How much did it cost you?"

"The price of a bottle of red wine."

"Didn't you know, woman, that this is insulation material that you use for lagging pipes?" said the the sergeant major, displaying his competence in this area as well.

"How am I s'posed to know that, sonny, when I've never had no education. There was thirteen of us in our family. I was the thirteenth," Granny said quietly.

And after all, how was she to know? And after all, she was number thirteen in the family. They span their thread by the light of a flare in their hut. Lived in the glade, turned the wheel as they prayed.

"Get her out of here. And don't let her ever cross my path again," said the groom, taking charge.

"Don't you start giving orders around here. We've put a roof over your head, so don't you start giving orders," said his father-in-law admonishingly. "Stop acting like a pig, stop yelling."

Shouts, noise.

"Who, me a pig?" said the groom indignantly. "Thanks very much, Dad. I'm asking you firmly once more to get Granny out of here.

Then the bride said: "Vasya! I love you, but I can't see her go. She used to feed me my porridge with a little spoon, and she was the one who took me to school the first day when I started in the first form of number ten Secondary School, which I left last year. Vasya! I love you, but she used to tell me fairy stories: the one about the peasant who deceived two generals and about the barrel of fish . . .

Shouts, noise.

"And we can quite easily tell you to clear off yourself," promised the father-in-law.

Shouts, noise. The accordions started playing.

"Vasya! You're strong, you're handsome. You can lift dumbbells. Vasya, forgive Granny."

But Vasya cast his sullen eyes over all those present and said: "All right! Then I'm going to the shop to get some matches because I want a smoke."

"I've got some matches! And some Belomor cigarettes! Have a smoke, pal," said the sergeant major coaxingly.

"No, I don't need anything that belongs to anyone else," answered the groom, and off he went to get some matches.

Off he went, and incidentally, he's never been seen since. They tried all manner of means to find him and eventually located him in the city of Norilsk, where he had flown to make a fast buck. He refused to come back, but explained that he was retaining his right to part of his bride's living space, seeing as he was her husband and he'd been given a work placement in the North.

So their love perished. It was sad, sad, comrades, it wasn't funny at all, as some of you might think. So their love perished and a family that hadn't even started was destroyed. And it was all because of stolen goods.

And the bride was left alone to grieve over her widow's lot, and she goes from one office to another trying in vain to get a divorce, and she is getting very embittered, seeing as these days it's not so easy for an honest girl to get divorced and to remarry. People are always talking about it and sometimes even the papers have something to say on the same matter.

So what am I talking to you about? Well, still about the same matter. So that you will treat with suspicion vendors like those who sell you crap on street corners. It's best not to get mixed up with them, and if you're not too lazy, take them straight to the police. My word of honour – it'll work out cheaper.

And most of all – don't go nicking stuff yourself. They'll catch you in the end! It'll be embarrassing! And altogether unpleasant. In actual fact we've got plenty of everything and our country is boundlessly rich, but after all you must have a conscience! Come to your senses, fellow countrymen! Be patient. Wait, my dear ones, for the bright future to arrive! After all, it's not a million miles away!

And then, whatever each of us wants, he can take. According to his needs, but within reason, of course, if I'm not getting something mixed up here.

# Strange Coincidences

"You see, what the fact of the matter is," said the chap I was talking to, a fellow by the name of Viktor. "The fact of the matter is that in our district there are a lot of elements who have the same surnames as famous people. They're not related to them, and actually, they're nobodies. But sometimes they disgrace their own surnames and the ones that are well-known by the things that they get up to."

"Strange coincidences," I said.

You see, we had one element here in our storehouse, a watchman he was, but he's not here anymore because he died recently. They buried him, and now he's lying in the ground on his own. They called him Uncle Lyonya Suvorov. Or was it Uncle Lyosha. I can't remember now. I think it was Uncle Lyosha. He was related to some boss in the town, who was working there as head of an economics research unit, and what do you think his surname was? Mazepa. His surname was Mazepa.

Well anyway, this selfsame Mazepa came out to our station once on business and dropped in to see Uncle Lyosha to have a word with him and sit down for a while. They sat at the table and had a bit to drink, and Uncle Lyosha complained to his relative that he earned very little money as a night watchman.

His relative fell deep in thought.

"I suppose you sleep when you're on duty, don't you?"he figured out at last.

"Well, of course I do. But that hasn't got anything to do with it. I'm on a fixed wage after all. I wouldn't earn any more if

I did the job properly. That's got nothing to do with it," Suvorov retorted justifiably.

"No it hasn't," said Mazepa.

"So tell me something I don't know," asked Uncle Lyosha.

And he waited. And for a long time Mazepa made no reply, since he was eating some stewed cabbage and pork. He finished the cabbage and wiped his greasy fingers on a serviette. Then he sighed and set about telling Suvorov something he didn't know.

"Oh, no. You mustn't sleep. A man who sleeps is a man who'll sleep through everything. Just you try not sleeping sometime when you're at your – not to put too fine a point on it – very humble post, and you'll see, your life will take a turn for the better.

"Well yeah, but," stuttered Uncle Lyosha, "I'm on a fixed wage, see."

"That's all there is to it. All there is to it. I've got nothing else to say to you. But you mark my words, a man who sleeps, is a man who'll sleep through everything. All the best, Alexei. Come and visit us sometime, I'm off to get my train now. All the best."

And off he went back to town.

Old Uncle Lyosha was flummoxed and couldn't make head or tail of it all. But, knowing that his relative was a clever and experienced man, he decided to put his trust in him and give it a try.

So on his very next night on duty he brewed himself up some *poluchifir*, drank it with a bit of sugar, and snuggled down in his sheepskin coat by the stores, cradling his gun in his arms so that the muzzle pointed towards the sky, to be precise, towards the constellation of the Great Bear.

Now, you see, despite the fact that it was pretty flimsy and didn't have decent locks or seals, their storehouse sometimes contained things that were absolutely essential for the proper management of the nation's economy.

In particular, it had just come to house some state-of-the-art glass blocks. These glass blocks were ribbed, greenish in colour and a bit bigger than a brick. I don't even know what their proper name was. I only know that they fix them in factory windows to reduce the noise out on the street that these firms make when they're working. You can also make walls out of them. And they're almost transparent. And of course, these glass blocks are also suitable, they're also suitable for use in the home, because everything is suitable for use in the home.

So right then. There was Uncle Lyosha, staying awake, admiring the stars, when he happened to notice that a car with its headlights turned off had pulled up at the store. And a hunched up man got out of the car, made straight for the storehouse, and made short work of its badly locked door.

"Stop! Or I'll shoot – is that what I'm s'pposed to say," Uncle Lyosha whispered to himself, getting the wind up, and then shouting: "Stop. Or I'll shoot! Where do you think you're going?"

But the hunched up man didn't say where he was going. He didn't say so, evidently because he considered the question a waste of time. And anyway, it was clear where he was going, and he couldn't have heard the question either, because by then he had long since disappeared into the recesses of the storehouse.

Well, time passed. Uncle Lyosha waited. And he waited until the other man came out. And he was even more hunched up now, seeing as he now had a weighty sack slung across his shoulders.

The stranger came close to the watchman and began swearing at him.

"What you shouting for, you old goat!"

However, you couldn't call him a stranger any longer, since Uncle Lyosha had no trouble in recognizing him as Alexander Alexandrovich Pushkin, the manager, about whom everyone in the firm used to say by way of a joke: "If you want that, you might as well ask Pushkin."

"I, I," said Uncle Lyosha, "I, I."

"You, you," said the stranger, now identified, mockingly. "You, you. Cat's got the flu."

And this made Uncle Lyosha pull himself together.

"Don't you use words like that," he said in a surly voice. "And don't try and make a joke out of it either. You'd better explain where you're making off to with this socialist property that I've been appointed to stand guard over for seventy roubles a month?"

"Ooh, don't he go on!"said Pushkin cheerfully. "Well done! Look after it! Be vigilant! Help yourself to half a sackful," he said, giving his permission, and ordered: "Well, go on then! Go on then! Back to your post!"

Then Uncle Lyosha helped him carry the sack the rest of the way to the car, and Pushkin drove off. He drove off, but for all that, this time he turned his headlights on.

Uncle Lyosha, happy man, put all the glass he'd been allowed into the sack, carried the sack out of the store, sat down on it and resumed his vigil, wide awake as could be.

And in actual fact, after the lapse of some time he heard the scraping noise of unoiled wheels, and a cart turned up. And that too was as quiet as quiet could be. Even quieter than the car.

The watchman, by now having acquired some experience in matters of this kind, didn't start yelling about shooting, but on the contrary kept quiet, as it were, and outwardly made it look as if he were asleep.

Well, the rest you know. Who should come out of the storehouse with a sackful of stuff but Pugachev, the foreman.

Pugachev the foreman was panting heavily under the weight of the sack, and Uncle Lyosha says to him imperiously: "Stop. No, stop. You're telling lies. Don't try anything on me. You won't get away."

And he rattled the bolt of his gun.

Pugachev dropped the sack from his broad shoulder and said in astonishment: "Is that you Uncle Lyosha? Ain't you asleep? Go to sleep, it's late."

"You should be ashamed of yourself, Fyodor. Put that sack back right away, or I'll shoot and make out a report. Maybe I'll lodge a complaint with Pushkin too. He and Kutuzov will show you the glass. You can see right through it."

"What are you on about, Suvorov?"retorted Pugachev. "Is this the way it is? Look, we're all people and we have to help one another, like brothers. You're probably not thinking straight because you're still half asleep. Eh? Own up, Uncle Lyosha.

You're not thinking straight, are you? You ought to get yourself admitted to the loony bin under Dr Plevaka."

To cut a long story short, they argued the toss for a long time, but then reached an agreement.

Pugachev off-loaded half a sack for Uncle Lyosha's benefit and rode off, feeling a bit peeved. So he took it out on the horse with the reins, shouting: "Get going, you bag of bones!"

But God loves threesomes, doesn't he? Isn't it true? Not half an hour had gone by before Uncle Lyosha was holding Vanka Zhukov the metal-worker by the collar, the namesake of that Zhukov who didn't know how to clean herring. Zhukov had been creeping into the storehouse.

"What am I to do with you? Eh? You know that I've only got to whistle, fire my gun, and you'll be doing hard labour. Do you want that?!"threatened Uncle Lyosha, gasping for breath after his struggle with Zhukov, who refused to be beaten.

"I'll smash your glasses, you old git," promised Zhukov.

"You can talk all you like. I'll have the book thrown at you. I'll have you doing hard labour," threatened Uncle Lyosha.

"Stop your chattering, and get out of my way."

"No, it's not on, Ivan," said Uncle Lyosha, turning more serious. "I've been appointed to stand here and stop people pilfering. If you want some of that glass, then I'd rather let you have you some of my own. I signed some out for myself today."

"How much?"

"Three roubles."

"How much glass, I'm asking."

"A sackful, that's how much."

"One sack's not enough. I owe Lomonosov alone that much.

"No. That's your lot. There isn't any more. I'm not allowing people to pilfer. So you're not taking any more away."

"Look, I'm a strong guy, I can carry them," implored Zhukov.

"No. That's your lot. You've got to know when to call it a day."

And Uncle Lyosha was adamant. Zhukov took the sack and went off, accompanying his departure with some choice swear words. He didn't have any money on him. He promised to pay later. Zhukov was an honest man.

And so Uncle Lyosha's life took on a new turn. Now he didn't sleep at night, he kept watch constantly. And he even achieved a number of successes, so he was able to buy himself a second-hand motorbike and side car. He did it up and got it going himself. He used to take the motorbike when he went to gather mushrooms, berries or nuts. The motorbike was a good runner and went very fast.

To put it in a nutshell, the namesakes plundered the whole storehouse.

And of course, in the end all their thieving and misappropriation was uncovered. There was a trial, and many of the namesakes were consequently dispatched to distant parts, to correct their mistakes.

Of the whole crew only Uncle Lyosha remained at home, because he set off at high speed on his motorbike, smashed into a BelAZ truck and killed himself. Did you know, a BelAZ is such a big vehicle? Just one of its wheels is twice the size of Uncle Lyosha's whole motorbike. So, as it happened, he died recently. They buried him and now he's lying alone in the earth.

"Strange coincidences," I said.

"Strange. And yet once, when he was still alive, he once came into town, called in at the economic research unit, went into the office, all lined with leatherette, where Mazepa was talking on a white telephone to someone.

He went in and said: "You were right, Mazepa."

And the latter replied: "I'm always right."

"Well done. I've brought you a present. A few glass blocks."

"What would I need them for? You can't make anything at home out of them, I've already tried. But anyway, seeing as you've brought them, let me have them."

And the two relatives went out into the street. The motorbike was parked there. But that's all that was there, the motorbike. The sack was no longer there. Thieves had stolen the sack. Uncle Lyosha was thoroughly upset and started patting the legs of his riding-breeches. And Mazepa said: "Damn it. There's a lot of thieves around these days . . ."

"Strange coincidences. Very strange. And why especially in your district? Perhaps there's something special about your district, eh? What do you mean?"I said, getting on at Viktor, when he'd finished his story.

"I don't mean anything. What are you trying to pin on me? Ours is just an ordinary district. Ordinary people. Good and bad. I've just told you about the bad ones, tomorrow I'll tell you about the good ones. It's an ordinary district, the only thing is this: by some strange coincidence there are a lot of elements living here who have the same surnames as famous people.

"Strange coincidences," I said, not giving up. "In my opinion, these elements should be invited to change their names by deed poll as a matter of urgency or their disgraceful actions should be curtailed and punished more severely.

"Yes, you could do it, of course. You could do all that, if the will was there," said Viktor.

# Miracles in a Jacket

Just imagine for a minute that you're not that highly organized person that you undoubtedly are in everyday life, but a young piss artist by the name of comrade Arkady Oskin.

So you get smashed out of your brains one night and start behaving accordingly. You're shouting, singing, dancing, and laughing your head off. And while you're dancing you try to turn your empty pockets inside out. The pockets get turned out and all the surrounding drunks testify to their absolute emptiness.

And then all of a sudden, next morning, your old jacket, hanging, abandoned on the back of a chair, affords you some unexpected surprises.

So then. This very same comrade Oskin, on waking up one morning, discovered nothing less than ten roubles in his very own jacket.

This occurrence astonished Arkady, because he hadn't had any money recently.

If you'll allow me to say it, this event really, really astonished Arkasha.

"It's a miracle," he said, staring stupidly at the money. "There are miracles in my tattered old jacket."

Having said "miracles" and having repeated the word "miracles", comrade Oskin got up from the bed to catch a fly that was aimlessly crawling over the window pane. Arkady threw the fly down on its back on the floor, crushed it under the hard heel of his shoe, put on his jacket and, still hung over, set off for work to do some honest toil and earn some money to live on.

Only he didn't make it to work, since he was an extraordinarily weak person. He met Fetisov. He showed him the ten roubles. The latter was also astonished. These best of pals talked about this and that, then turned off to you know where – and you know the rest.

So in fact, comrade Oskin came home late that night singing a Ukrainian folk song called "She planted cucumbers by the water". He sang for a bit and then collapsed into bed with his clothes on.

When he woke up the next morning he felt really quite amazed at the absurdity of his life.

"What are you doing, you scoundrel?" said Arkady, standing in front of the mirror and not recognizing himself. "It'll all end with me sinking straight to the bottom and getting the sack from work."

"And quite right too," said a Voice.

"Hardly quite right too," objected Arkady. "After all, I'm a human being. A human being. Do you understand me?"

And he carried on muttering something to himself, running his hands over himself and the clothes he hadn't taken off.

Then he had to twig himself by the nose, because there was no other thing for it. Because in the very same pocket of the very same jacket he found the very same, or maybe different, ten roubles, the same ten-rouble note, the same red banknote!

"Ooh," said Arkady, "Ooh, what's going on! I don't understand it and I'm scared."

He said that and looked from side to side wildly.

But either side of him there were only bare walls. There was almost nothing on the walls. He was always telling everybody, of course, that he didn't need anything, but he was lying, the rascal.

Gazing around wildly from side to side, comrade Oskin went out into the street, but he didn't understand anything there either.

The trams were running. People he knew were walking by. The shops were selling food and drink.

To cut a long story short, he came home very late again that night, and this was how the young man stood on the ground: with his feet at ninety degrees to each other, rocking backwards and forwards, from heel to toe, from toe to heel.

"Oh, comrade Oskin! Could you really have drunk your way right through ten roubles, even if you don't know how you found it?" asked the Voice.

But the poor lad didn't reply. He had masses of questions of his own which demanded immediate answers.

"What's going to happen?" enquired Oskin, in fear and despair kneading his white fingers. "Can this really be happening?"

And naturally, he didn't find out if it could or not. And how could it be otherwise? After all, he was in the room on his own, who could answer him? The Voice? But the Voice itself didn't know what was what.

After his hysterics, exclamations and questions, comrade Oskin woke up – obviously once again with a hangover – but this time a fairly composed man. With a practised hand he felt in his pocket. He no longer kneaded his fingers, he was no longer astonished, he merely gasped with pleasure to see the ten roubles in its usual place.

He got up, went out, walked off, enjoyed himself, went back to bed, slept. Drunk.

A new day. The old story. The same jacket. The same ten-rouble note. Take the ten-rouble note. Off he goes, well pleased.

"Oh, Oskin, Oskin," calls the Voice after him. "You'll come to no good . . ."

Yet he couldn't give a toss for the Voice.

And there's no such thing as miracles. I draw your attention to this indisputable fact, given that on the fifth day of finding these sums of money comrade Oskin discovered not ten roubles, but a total of only seven roubles. And seven roubles isn't ten roubles.

And things went from bad to worse. On the sixth day there were only three roubles all told. A three-rouble note. He drank it away.

Then the seventh day of this week of miracles arrived. And on this seventh day of his week of miracles comrade Oskin felt in his miraculous jacket and pulled out six copper kopecks.

Now one ought to note that by some strange coincidence this seventh day was a Monday. And as everyone knows, Monday is the start of the working week.

Now although Oskin was a piss artist, he was no fool. He knew what you could do, and what you couldn't. He knew that you could miss work for a week, but that after that, you wouldn't have a job to go back to.

Oskin, no fool, looked at the clock. The clock had stopped. Oskin, no fool, turned on the radio. "Morning exercises! Morning exercises!"

And Oskin realized that he wasn't late for work, and that if he hurried, he might be in time. He could still go to work.

He grabbed a quick bite to eat, just gulped something down there in the kitchen, cleaned his boots, smoothed down his thinning hair, got on a bus with his six kopecks and arrived at work.

At work comrade Oskin explained rather hastily to the enquiring management that for the five working days of the previous week he had been at the bedside of his sick grandfather, who had been semiconscious. Now his grandfather had died, and comrade Oskin was back at work, and was requesting that he be signed in retrospectively somehow, bearing in mind the loss of his grandfather, or be granted a holiday retrospectively, at his own expense, if they couldn't take into account the loss of his grandfather.

This is how the scene unfolded further.

"It's very sad, comrade Oskin, that your grandfather has died. There's one less splendid fellow in the world. May his memory rest eternal in our hearts. But would you be so kind as to tell us what happened to the sixty roubles six kopecks of trade union funds which were entrusted to you to be paid in?"

At this comrade Oskin lowered his eyes and wept bitter, bitter tears.

"Comrades," he said. "If only I were the only guilty party! But it runs in our family, you know. My dad Vasily used to drink a lot of vodka. And grandfather Prof did too. And great grandfather Stepan drank so much that he ended up sitting on the stove all the time, eating uncooked dough. Comrades! Collective of workers! Help me if you can. Help me, and I'll pay the money back later."

"He's right. He is guilty, but not to the extent that he could be punished harshly for what he's done," said the collective of workers who had been convened, and they helped comrade Oskin.

They sent him off for compulsory alcoholic treatment to a splendid clinic, full of light, air and the smell of conifers.

Oskin emerged from there looking younger and clear-headed. He's a sight to behold. He no longer keeps finding money in his jacket, since now he's got a different jacket, a new one, and he keeps all his money in the bank.

Oskin no longer weeps. He doesn't hold conversations with the Voice, he doesn't catch devils or crush flies and he doesn't shout "What is to be done?" Now he knows himself what has got to be done. Avoid miracles of the kind described above, that's what's got to be done.

For they rarely lead to a happy end, and if they do, then only in stories that are the spitting image of this one.

# The Mistakes of Youth

Once when I was coming home in the dead of night, I was bloodily beaten up by some people who at first I took to be hooligans and criminals.

But they didn't take me for just anyone, but very much the one they were after.

I was walking along, and they were standing in the entrance to a block of flats. It was my entrance, and they were waiting between the ground floor and the first floor.

They stood there and said: "Listen, mate, have you got a smoke?"

I did, and handed over. They lit up and went on: "Listen, mate, have you got a clear conscience?"

With a ready smile I was about to joke that I didn't have a clear conscience, and that in my opinion there were no people left like that who did have a clear conscience.

But I didn't have time to make the witticism, because they gave my face a re-eal bashing, one-two, left-right, me seeing stars.

Well, what could I do? I kept quiet, swallowed it. There was a lot of them and I was on my own.

"Is that it?" I said. "Or is there going to be any more?"

There were five of them. One of them started snarling outright.

"Let go of him," he shouted, "I'm going to cripple him now . . ."

And the others tried to dissuade him. They said: "Take it easy, Seryozha. Don't worry. We'll have a word with him. He'll get what's coming to him now, the lousy bastard. Don't you worry!"

By now Seryozha was grinding his teeth.

Grinding his teeth, and yet I was surprised as to why they were so worked up, shouting and making a racket. Instead of doing their business quietly, robbing me in silence, they were making a performance of it.

"You got a clear conscience?"

"Yes, I have. You're wasting your time, lads. I haven't got a watch, because it's already been stolen, had it cut off my wrist. Who needed it?"

"Shut up! So you've got a clear conscience, have you? So how come Lena drank vinegar concentrate? That was nothing to do with you, was it? Well? It's got nothing to do with you, has it? Oh, you bastard!"

Then they really started laying into me.

"Oh, Jesus Christ," I thought. As long as I can keep on my feet. Otherwise they'll put the boot in. They'll chew me up. Make mincemeat of me . . ."

"What's this all about?" I shouted.

"You know, you know what it's all about. Hit him, mates!"

"I don't know, honest I don't know."

I have to say that this was all going on in almost complete darkness, since in the first place it was night, and in the second place there are never any light bulbs in our entrance. It was dark. There was a moon.

Well, they kept hitting me, hitting me. Lights flashing in my eyes, I was seeing stars.

Then they got tired of thumping me. And I could see they were tired, I fell down on the floor, groaning softly now and then, pitifully. After all, it hurt.

Well, then they decided to light a match and have a look at me, to see if I had got what was coming to me or whether I deserved a bit more.

They lit the place up and saw that they'd got the wrong person.

At that they wanted to run away, and they did even run a little way down one flight of stairs, but then they changed their minds. They came back, stopped and stood there.

"Look mate," they said. "We don't know what to say to you. It was bad luck, it was a terrible mistake. We got you mixed up with somebody else. We took you for someone else, some rat."

"Ooh, I'm still gonna find him, I'm, I'm, I'm still gonna find him," said Seryozha.

"No, I'm not going to leave it at that," I said. "I'm going to have you up in court, you criminals."

"You can take us to court. You can. We won't protest. When something bad like this has happened, then we're going to have to answer for it, but try to understand . . ."

I ran my hands over my body. I ran my hands over my body and stood up. My teeth were still there, but my lip was swollen, and my sides hurt . . ."

"But what's this all about? Why?" I said.

"Just try to understand. We mistook you for someone else . . ."

"Ooh, how could I get the wrong one!" howled Seryozha.

"Try to understand. There's this guy. Then our Lena, she's from round our way, she's in our work-team. And he's a rat. It turns out he's got a wife, and a kid.

"Really," I said in surprise. "Is there really a scoundrel like that living in our block?"

"Yes, there is, there is. Block fourteen, flat thirteen. They told us that he wasn't at home. Out gallivanting. Again. The bastard."

"Ah," I thought, "It's all right then. It's true that our block was number sixteen, not fourteen, but what's the difference, if Lena . . . True, I'd never had a Lena, but what was the difference, if Lena . . . It was a bad business. And so, apparently, nobody here had anything to do with it. What the hell? What was going on?"

"He promised to marry her. She used to go out with Seryozha. But he promised to marry her, so she gave Seryozha the push. Ooh, the bastard!"

"I'll get him, I'll get him," said Seryozha, "Don't you worry!"

"How many rascals are there like that in the world? Who needs them! Give us a smoke," I said, licking my injured lip.

. . . and the bruises on my face became suffused with a miraculous blue light, and my grazes started to dry out a bit, and the pain eased.

Once again life seemed splendid and astonishing. I turned out not to be the one they were after. The mistakes of youth. I wanted to shout for the joy of existing, but I couldn't, for it was the dead of night outside. It was dark.

# No Cinema

"By the way, talking about the cinema. You know, it's really surprising, I'm so fond of the arts that I still go to the cinema, and last year I even went to a musical comedy," said Galibutaev, taking off his mittens and lighting a Wave cigarette.

We were surprised and asked him to tell us about it.

Galibutaev kept refusing. He shouted that the working day wasn't over yet for him to go blathering on. That it wasn't even the lunch break yet for him to be telling stories. That a break for a smoke shouldn't last more than five minutes. That was the rules. And that he needed more time than that for his story.

Only there was no saying when Galibutaev would stop once he'd opened his mouth. And so he began.

The fact of the matter is that I'm very fond of all sorts of films and plays. That's the fact of the matter. And so last year when they put up a notice in our club to say that the film of *The Lower Depths*, a two-reeler, was coming and it was going to be on at six and nine o'clock in the evening, I made up my mind that I would definitely be there.

Only I didn't know at that time who had written the play. I know now that it's a play by Maxim Gorky, but at the time I thought it was by Chekhov and Turgenev. And that was all because I had rotten teachers at school.

So I got to the club just before nine o'clock, so as not to have to wait, and what do I see?

I see that it looks as if the film isn't about to begin.

All around there are people playing table tennis, drunks staggering about and girls cracking sunflowers seeds.

I asked the manager if the showing was going to start soon, and he replied almost insolently: "I'm afraid that you're wasting your time."

"Why?" I enquired almost politely.

"Because," explained the manager more insolently, and he was the projectionist as well, "I can't be bothered to show the film just for one person."

"What!" I said indignantly. "Am I really the only one to come and see a brilliant play by Chekhov and Turgenev. "Those people playing table tennis, those drunks staggering around in the corners there, the ones cracking sunflower seeds, don't you think they make up an audience?"

"Whatever they are, they're not such far-gone idiots as to pay forty kopecks each to see something they don't know, even if it is brilliant. And by the way, this play is not by Chekhov and Turgenev, but by Gorky. Which just goes to show that you're no expert either, but that you don't wanna find something else to do, or you can't find something else to do."

He really had a go at me, but I just calmly stuck to my guns: "Well what should I do then? Why did you put up that notice that got me all excited and urged me to come and see a brilliant work, even if it was by Gorky?"

"It's got nothing to do with me," said the manager chirpily. "You write a letter to the rental people telling them to send us films that will draw audiences in, not send them running to hide in corners."

"What sort of films have you got in mind?"

"Well, something like *Flowers in the Dust*. Every last one of them saw that. And you'd watch it too."

"*Divorce Italian Style*, what about that?"

"No," said the manager more seriously. "Divorce didn't make anything at the box office here. Why that was, I don't know myself. There was even some capitalist debauchery in it, but it never made good box office. I don't know."

"So, no cinema then." I said, spelling it out.

"I've already told you – write a letter to the film rental people," said the manager, taking offence. "Or get an audience together yourself. You need at least fifteen people."

"Is that the law or something?" I asked.

"Yes, it's the law, it's the law. For a one-reel film no less than five people, and for a two-reeler, not less than fifteen."

"Shouldn't that be the other way round?"

"Do you think I don't know the law or something?"

"That's strange. That's a very strange law. I've never heard of a law like that before," I said, and went off to try and collect an audience.

"Citizens," I said, "Let's all go and see this film *The Lower Depths* by the brilliant writer Gorky."

I said it a second time, but no one heard me.

Then I went over to the table-tennis table.

"Are you going to watch the film?"

"No," said one player with a wispy moustache, answering for all of them, and shouted: "Love all! Your serve!"

I went over to the girls, and they were giggling.

"You'll have to study this at school one day, you silly tarts!" I shouted.

And one of them announced: "We've already learnt everything for ourselves."

"Maybe we can teach you a thing or two."

"It's just awful," I replied. "It's just awful what the youth of today is coming to."

And I didn't even bother to try the staggering drunks, because that was just what they were waiting for, for me to try them.

I didn't bother to try them, they started themselves, one of them shouting at me: "Oy, you, Luka-the-Comforter from Gorky's novel *The Mother*!"

Why should I want to talk to a drunk?

I went back to the manager and told him, more or less, what they'd told me.

"There you are," laughed the manager. "No people, so no cinema."

"Then perhaps you could show it tomorrow, seeing as it's a great film?"

"Yes, if there's fifteen of you."

"Fifteen men on a dead man's chest!" bellowed the drunk who had called me Luka-the-Comforter, who happened to be standing near by.

It was a strange law. Why fifteen exactly, and not ten, for example?

"So what's going on in the club today?"

"What's going on in the club today is anything that you organize for yourselves. If the lads bring an accordion, there can be dancing, and if they don't bring one, then there won't be any dancing, and I'm going home."

"But it's going to hit you in the pocket, isn't it, if the film doesn't get shown?" I said.

"No, it won't, my dear chap. It won't hit me in the pocket," said the manager, as nice as pie. "It won't hit me in the pocket, my old pal, because my earnings don't depend on the receipts, I get a regular wage."

"What about bonuses?"

"I never get bonuses, so I've got nothing to lose."

Now that ought to have put Galibutaev down once and for all. But no chance. Galibutaev was not the sort of guy to be put down once and for all. Of course, he was no god, tsar or hero, and it was possible to break him, but not right away. And there was no bending him either.

"What's the minimum number of people necessary to keep you sitting in the hall?"

"I've told you. For a one-reeler five, for a two-reeler fifteen."

"Okay. Let me have fifteen tickets. Forty kopecks each. That'll be six roubles. I'll pay."

At first the manager hesitated a bit, or to be more precise, he didn't hesitate at all. He took six roubles off me, which was just about all I had left until payday (but that's not important) and shouted: "The film's starting, the cinema's open!"

And I said: "If anyone wants to go in for free, I'll let them."

They jumped at the chance of going in for free. There was some old woman, deaf and blind, and no doubt poor; the big-mouth who'd just been shouting his head off about fifteen dead men; and then various blokes and girls. They were giggling.

I won't tell you what the play *The Lower Depths* is about, said Galibutaev, continuing his story. You all know it well. At least you ought to know it better than me, since you were all good at school, whereas I was brought up in a children's home, where I was forced to eat mustard as a punishment for smoking in the toilets. You all know it, so I'm not going to go over it again for you.

But you should have seen the way the actors performed. Ooh! Aah! There was one who plays the part of the ACTOR in the play. He's a very nice man and says that he suffers from "halkohol", not alcohol. Then he hangs himself.

Then there's Luka – he's a sharp one too. A good man. I can't remember the name of the actor who played him. The whole film was really good. It showed all the futility of the situation in tsarist Russia.

I couldn't take my eyes off it, but you could hear the ping pong balls in the foyer outside banging away. Well, all right then. It wasn't that noisy, but it did interfere a bit with you watching the film, but it wasn't that noisy.

Then suddenly a concertina started up! No, not in the film, no. In the foyer. And then some bastards started shuffling their feet. And then someone started squawking:

*Said he'd lost his papers, that he did,*
*He still had to pay maintenance for the kid,*
*Thirty-three kopecks in every rouble.*
*Oh, yeah.*

At that I charged out of the hall and yelled: "Stop making that noise! Can't you see there's a film on here!"

And the manager-projectionist also came out of his box and ordered: "Oy, you lot, shoo! Keep the noise down. There's a film on."

"What film's that then. Thirty-three kopecks in every rouble. They show all sorts of rubbish," yelled the drunk who I'd let in on my hard-earned cash, as he came rolling out of the hall.

"Shh," said the manager to him.

I went back into the hall, where the lads and the girls were sitting with their arms round each other, not budging, and the old woman was snoozing sweetly.

I sat down in the front row to get a proper look at what was happening next.

They were all out in the yard. Bubnov kept looking out of the window, Nastya was reading a novel, and Luka was preparing to make himself scarce. The baron was swaggering about.

Only at that point the lads and the girls behind me suddenly started having a row. At first quietly, but then one lad shouted: "I'll smack you in the gob, you bitch, and then you'll do as you're told."

And the bitch replied: "Go on then. And I'll get you fifteen days inside. Go on, just you try it."

At first it was quiet, but then it got louder and louder. And then in the film Natasha scalded her legs. It was such a touching scene. I completely lost my temper. I turned round and asked them: "Quiet, will you be quiet."

I just couldn't understand that lad, it was all out of irritation. Just out of irritation that lad said to me: "Shut up."

And the girl said as well: "You shut up, Veryovkin."

Smoking a cigarette, she was. The hussy.

Then I started to lay my tongue to everything. The manager came in and said officially: "All those smoking will have to leave the auditorium."

And they all said: "No one's smoking."

But the boss threw them all out. They said that they would settle my hash. They were drunks, so I can understand them. And the manager said that he had had nothing but trouble from me, and that if only he had known, he wouldn't have had anything to do with me.

So anyway, I was left to watch the rest of *The Lower Depths*. The concertina was squeaking away in the foyer, shoe soles were scraping the floor, there was shouting in the foyer, but I wasn't going to interfere any more. Damn them. I was going to sit there, and watch the rest of the film. All on my own, if you didn't count the old woman asleep there.

Damn! When they started singing "The Sun Rises and Sets", it brought tears to my eyes.

But then the manager turned the lights up. The picture was over.

And I went out into the street.

It was dark there. Damn. Couldn't see a thing!

I would have turned a torch on, but I didn't have one with me.

It was dark, and there were some cars parked there. The cars were parked and I was on foot.

And then three guys came out from behind one of the cars and said: "Take that, you bastard!"

And they started thumping me.

But after all, Galibutaev's no fool either. I had a half-bottle stashed way in reserve, and as soon as I belted one of them with that, he went straight down."

And Galibutaev laughed happily. He took off his hat and wiped his sweaty bald head.

"At this point, I felt really pleased with myself, and thought that I had practically won. Only my pleasure was a little premature, because one of them ran over to the car. He came back. And it was so neat and so hard the way he hit me on the head with the tyre lever that I fell down, covered in blood. Then they gave me a bit of a kicking, before running off.

And I was left lying there until some good people came along and helped me up.

"And what happened then?"

"What happened then? I was telling you about the cinema. That's what makes all this so surprising that I'm still so very fond of the arts. I love going to the cinema, and last year I even went to a musical comedy. They soon caught the people who did it, after I was helped up, and now they're where they belong, doing hard labour. And I got mentioned in the paper, on the 'Court Cases' page, where they said that I'd put up a good show and hadn't been afraid of that gang of hooligans."

"Oh, that's just typical of you, Galibutaev, a lot of hogwash, don't give us that bullshit," said someone.

"I'm not. The only thing I don't know is whether there really is a law that says that if you haven't got fifteen people, then there won't be any cinema. Maybe the manager just dreamed that one up, just cooked it up himself. At least, that's the way it seems to me," said Galibutaev quietly and put on his mittens again.

The break for a smoke was over.

# The Higher Wisdom

". . . For caution is the higher wisdom," he realized.

This is what had happened.

He was travelling on a trolley bus, it was overcrowded was this trolley bus, and so that his black buttons didn't get torn off in the crush of people, he decided to lean against the trolley bus exit (actually it was the entrance).

Now the conductress, an experienced lady, happened to notice this action of his in the thick of the crowd, and she shouted out in her shrill, her trained conductor's voice, which was to be heard above the roar of the passengers: "Don't lean, on no account lean, against the trolley-bus doors, one man has leant against them once today already and he fell out on the street!"

That dear, kind, elderly conductress! Slowly he detached himself, of course, from the door.

And the trolley bus went quiet, because everyone felt scared.

"Well, what happened to . . . him?" asked someone who could not be seen behind the backs and torsos and heads, trying not to betray the agitation in his voice. "What happened to him?"

"Oh, nothing," answered the conductress, also quietly for some reason, "Nothing happened to him, nothing at all. Vasya put the brake on, we ran back to him, turned him over, lifted him up, and there he was – dead drunk, he climbed back in the bus, and all the way to the terminus kept effing and blinding at the lot of us . . ."

The passengers livened up, blossomed even.

"Yes . . . It happens . . ."

"As they say, it's water off a duck's back to someone who's drunk."

"If'n he'd bin sober, he woulda killed 'imself, he woulda been smashed to bits . . ."

"Don't you talk like that right in my face."

"Well, if'n yer don't like it, yer can find yerself a taxi and ride in that."

And, on hearing the word "taxi", someone who was sitting down, unshaven and red-eyed, closed his red eyes and turned to the window.

"You're a bit out of date, by the way, citizen, answering back like that about taxis. 'Cos as it happens, they've been talking about all this in the newspapers, and decided that you mustn't answer back like that, that you have to behave yourself more decently on public transport."

And so the usual scene that took place and always takes place on this over-crowded trolley bus was resumed and went its way.

But it's all the same – nice, dear, nice, kind comrade conductress!

After all, maybe you don't know, well probably you don't know, but he's never again going to lean against the doors on public transport . . .

". . . for caution is the higher wisdom. Just behave like everyone else and as your experience of life prompts you, and you'll live to see your grey hairs and you'll die a natural death," he realized.

Okay. But that's not the end yet.

He got off the trolley bus. His black buttons were in tact. His money was in tact. Only he'd lost a fur glove. Oh dear, dear, dear! Walking into work, he grieved: "What a fine glove that was – leather on the outside, fur on the inside. Warm. Hot. I'm going to be lost without it in frosts like this, frosts so cold you could spit at someone and not only would he be offended, he would also get hurt because the spit would turn to ice on the way. Farewell, my unfortunate glove! I'll freeze now, like a dog. I'll get gangrene in my right hand, and by spring I'll have to have my right hand amputated . . ."

He fell deep in thought, grieving. Walking into work, he grieved. Suddenly there was a shout: "Hang on a minute, luv! . . ."

And some old woman he didn't know came hurrying through the winter snow drifts towards him.

"Where you running off to, ducks?"

To start with, he wanted to say something nasty to the old

woman, but something that she wouldn't understand, something like "to the cemetery", or "to the baths", he wanted to say something nasty because he was still very miserable about losing his glove, but he restrained himself, and just said brusquely to the old crone: "To the factory, missus, where else?"

"Are you going any further along this path?" The old woman's cheeks, her eyelids had red veins all around them, and tears came to her eyes – because of the wind, because of her old age, because of her incomprehensible concern about him.

"Yes, I am going further along this path, missus, I am, there are plenty of idiots these days who want to go wading through snow drifts . . ."

"And have you had a little spot of vodka today, have you?"

"I never touch the stuff, old woman. Not vodka, not wine, not beer, not cognac – I don't drink anything, never go near it."

"Is that the truth?"

"Absolutely. I have a liver problem, old girl."

"Then Christ be with you, then go on your way, dear one," stated the old woman drily, and was about to plunge back into the snow drifts.

But at that point he lost his temper, got furious, grabbed her by the flap of her coat. He pressed her: "Look old woman, why are you winding me up like this?"

"I'm not winding you up, I was just trying to save you," answered the old woman with dignity. "You got any idea what'll be waiting for you up ahead?"

And up ahead, it must be said, there was a transformer box and a post by the box, a wooden one, with a bracket on it which looked like a giant letter "L".

And the old woman explained to him that if anyone who had been drinking vodka walked under that big electrified letter, then he'd immediately be killed by an electric shock. This folk superstition, she said, had a basis in physics, since the electromagnetic field, acting in conjunction with the enhanced gamma rays of the sun, determines the internal structure of the alcohol found in the human organism – the alcohol instantly cools to a temperature of minus ten degrees Celsius, you fall down dead and immobile, and there is nothing that can revive you.

You dear, kind, dear, kind, sweet old soul! Maybe you don't know, well probably you don't know, yet now he's never going to walk under ominous protuberances like that again and he's never going to drink vodka . . .

". . . for caution is the higher wisdom. Look after yourself and spot the unpleasant and the dangerous, and you'll live far into a good future," he realized.

But that's not everything yet. It's not the end of the story yet, since basically, it comes in three parts, and for my character to become fully established in his wisdom, he has to encounter yet another incident, which will confirm the validity of his higher wisdom – a third incident.

He didn't have to wait long. Apparently, he was destined to become acquainted with everything associated with the higher wisdom all in one day.

No sooner had he got to the factory, no sooner had he sat down at his desk to do some work, than the boss said to him: "Let's go out into the corridor, Alexander Petrovich, I've been sent some cigarettes from Moscow, Bulgarian ones."

"What are they called?" he asked.

"They're called Phoenix" replied his boss. "They're brand new cigarettes, which Bulgaria didn't use to export to us before. I was in Moscow in – I can't remember when exactly, about 1965, I think – and I went to a Bulgarian exhibition. And even there I didn't see cigarettes like these, though they had all sorts and varieties on display, like Shipka, Sun, Balkan, Bulgartabak, Rila, Derby, and lots of others, which, to tell you the truth, I can't altogether recall now, but I know for sure that they didn't have Phoenix there, I think."

They went out into the corridor, allegedly to have a smoke, but instead he heard the following remarkable words from his boss: "Look here. If you're late for work once more, you sod, then I'll have you writing a letter of explanation. I couldn't care less myself about your lateness, because though you're not the best worker in the world, you know your job, and at least you cope with it. But if by chance the management carries out a check, then you and I and all of us will lose our quarterly bonuses and then I'll really be furious and I'll tear you to pieces because of the money and authority I'll have lost, you whoreson. Understand?"

And in reply – actually, instead of replying – he just went and kissed the boss on the forehead.

The boss was at a complete loss, but he explained his actions as follows: "My dear, kind, dear, kind boss, dear Yury Mikhailovich. I'm not just grateful to you for the fact that now I will get up an hour earlier and get to work before the cleaners have even washed the floors in the corridors, so as not to be late. The main thing is that I am also grateful to you for the fact that now I am completely established in my new-found wisdom, and I realize that caution is the higher wisdom! Live honestly, live cautiously, live quietly and nicely, observe the rules – and everyone will like you and you'll live to see your own grey hairs, and you'll die a natural death in a good future!

And just imagine, the boss agreed with him, because this was something that one could not disagree with.

And now he lives as if he were in heaven and, having passed through purgatory, is heading for paradise.

Everyone respects him. He has more money. He has joined the Hunters' and Fishers' Society and last summer when he was out with them he shot a hazelhen with a double-barrelled shotgun. It was delicious!

I for my part, like everyone else, greatly respect this character, or more exactly, this man who is almost the hero of my story – there, you see, I have written an artistic work, consisting entirely of his life's experience.

I've written it, and what do you think, should I send it off somewhere to be published?

No, no-o! For caution is the higher wisdom. My hero remembers this, and I know it too.

Let this story rather lie at home in my grandfather's trunk, sealed on his orders, for the edification of my future descendents, so that they, when I have departed for a better world, will read it, weep, and say: "In truth our daddy was a very wise man!"

# Pork Kebabs

All sorts of people used to come to the cosy little restaurant at Poddelkovo Station on the Moscow railway line, all sorts of people used to sit there for minutes, hours and days, all sorts, but always good people.

And the station itself was, well, absolutely beautiful – a real gem. The station had a polished, middle-sized bell, bronze, which was never rung, and there was also an antique clock there with rigid hands and embossed numerals on its face, and there was also an attendant in a red cap – stern and aloof, whereas the station policeman was just the opposite; Yashka the blue-capped cop was a very unassuming and accessible personality: sometimes he even used the butt of his revolver to crack walnuts for the kids.

And the Moscow-Volga Canal came so close by to the station, that in the summer you could see the deck of the motor ship full of merry optimists, and the empty expanse of a passing barge's upper deck, where sailors' washing was fluttering in the breeze and barefoot figures, installed amid the stacks of ready-cut firewood, executed popular songs and dances to the accompaniment of miniature accordions – most often "I Have Never Been", the same number that Muslim Magomaev, the opera and variety singer, performs.

And the suburban electric trains – whoom-whoom – long grey rats throwing grey shadows onto the grey asphalted platform; psst-psst go the rubberized doors, and then chug-chug, they're on their way to Moscow.

Yes, yes. That's it, to Moscow, and nowhere else, because this station was the terminus for the suburban trains, so if anyone wanted to go further than this from Moscow, then he was obliged to get on an old-fashioned steam train with its ticket collector, its supply of boiling water for tea, its steam engine, funnel and smoke, and ordinary people really did get on such trains – more often than not carrying man-made fibre suitcases and knapsacks – and they set off for who knows where – either to Petersburg, which was not so far away, or to Vorkuta: in a word, this was a northern route, not one that led to any warm countries.

Right then. Now, the district adjoining the station had roots that stretched back into untamed antiquity, when the Tartars were stronger than the Russians and the people built fortresses with monasteries inside, with ramparts, moats and sturdy gates to keep the Tartars out. Naturally, building the fortresses was a waste of time, but the benefit was felt a few centuries later when "The Fortress and Monastery of Poddelkovo" acquired a "State Preservation Order" as a monument to ancient culture and to the racial characteristics of the inhabitants of Poddelkovo district, in whom, as in a drop of water, there was partially reflected the hotly disputed thesis propounded by certain comrades, that there are no Russians left in Russia and that we are all half-breeds, and anyone who calls himself a Russian and asserts that he was born of a Russian woman, is lying through his teeth or is simply mistaken, having failed to grasp the essence of the question, or having ignored it completely.

Obviously the district, possessing such a quantity of reliques of Russian antiquity in its main town and everywhere else, could not be so far advanced as regards its industrial development, but our district's strong point was in its erudition: in addition to its scientific research institutes housed in the cellars of the churches, where archivists burrowed away, having graduated from the Moscow Institute of Historical Archives, there was also in commission an enormous atomic power station for peaceful purposes, replacing the need for peat, coal, petrol, solar power, and firewood, and requiring only water, graphite and a little bit of uranium-235. And the macrobiological station with its guinea pigs, dolphins, turtles and dogs was so famous throughout the world that frequently the streets of this ancient, and consequently somewhat tedious, little town, were enlivened by the presence of foreigners – people looking exactly like us, but not understanding a word of Russian.

There's no need to tell you about the technical colleges, the Plant and Factory Colleges, the institutes, the Schools for Young Workers. It's obvious, we've got masses of them. I'll just mention – before I come to the main events of my sad story – one other place of note in the district: the open psychoneurological clinic with its twelve hundred beds. This also made a reputation for itself throughout the Soviet Union, because there they introduced new medicines, new methods of treatment and residential care for patients, and moreover, the air, the air around Moscow, unique by virtue of its chemical properties, together with the forest and the proximity of calm water straightened out in no time at all the over-convoluted minds of those people suffering, alas, from ailments all too common in our intelligent age.

And the latest of the methods which the medics thought up was this: CPC – a Community Patients' Council.

And the patients were so pleased at this that they immediately initiated the publication of a wall newspaper in a print run of two copies with the title of *For a Healthy Mind*, where boldly, but cautiously, they criticized individual orderlies for their occasional uncaring behaviour, and after the publication of the newspaper they went even further – they themselves, cheerfully and singing away, redecorated the whole hospital and painted it out in bright blue, a joy to behold, so that the psychoneurological clinic became one of the most conspicuously beautiful buildings of the town, but that wasn't important – the important thing was that the work cured many of the permanent residents of the hospital completely, once and for all, with the result that there were somewhat fewer of them than one thousand two hundred, and so some beds were left empty; and the work etched a certain wisdom and tranquillity on the others, which allowed them to cope with their abnormal condition more easily. Look what a salutary contribution could be made to the healing process by the Community Council and by a bit of hard work!

You can see for yourself, dear reader, my friend and foe, what riches the Poddelkovo Station and its adjoining district have to offer the novice writer in the way of subject matter and plots. But I'm not going to write about the magical activity of the atom, nor about guinea pigs, nor about antiquity, nor about madmen. I prefer something simpler, as the song goes, reader! After all, so far there's been no end to the sad incidents which give rise to sad stories, like the one described below, yet when they do come to an end, then I'll write about the other things, about archivists and happy-go-lucky students. So don't be angry, just read on, and hear my sad story about the little restaurant at Poddelkovo Station, called simply the Poddelkovo, about the dramatic events that took place within its walls and in the district court afterwards, and then at the assizes in front of the state prosecutor, three correspondents from various newspapers and a throng of excited members of the public.

Now this little restaurant was situated right inside the railway station. To get to it you had to push open the stiff station entrance door, cross a room containing yellow wooden benches on which travellers dozed, and where in addition to everything else there was a pay phone, from which, for fifteen kopecks, you could ring the centre direct, Moscow – the heart of Russia. And then you had to open yet another door, a glass door with a doorman in attendance, and then go over to a table and sit down and savour the aroma of that one dish which everyone came here to sample – namely, the "Pork Kebabs", the restaurant's pride and joy, its very own creation, or if one were to be precise and objective, the creation of its manager, the inimitable and highly talented Oleg Alexandrovich Svidersky, about whom I will tell all, but not till a little later on, because first I must tell you about the kebabs, because it was they which were the spark that set the whole forest on fire.

Among the numerous prime qualities the kebabs displayed, the chief ones stood out sharply: the relatively moderate price per portion and the unforgettable taste. Well, you judge for yourselves, you crackpots, where else might you get, within the vicinity of Moscow, and at a price of sixty-four kopecks, such pieces of real meat, tempting both to the eye and the palate, served with a spicy orange-coloured sauce, and garnished with a little onion, or sometimes even a slice of lemon! Ah! The mere process of committing to paper the recollections those gustatory sensations which he has experienced fills the mouth of the person writing these lines with rich, thick saliva.

"The main thing about it is that the portions are such a decent size, oh, such a decent size, just amazing," those who understood would say nervously, as they checked with a moist eye that Nelly, the waitress, was unloading the steel plates properly from the steel serving tray onto the neatly laid table, which sported beer bottles and SMP (salt, mustard, pepper) cruet sets.

And those understanding persons became nervous not for any objective reasons, but because they were drinking vodka that they had smuggled in from the state liquor store, not the restaurant's vodka, for as everyone knows, buying vodka in a restaurant is extraordinarily expensive. Moreover, if the representative of the management in the person of a waiter noticed that the restaurant's interests were being undermined in the interests of the state liquor store's, he would promptly, though clandestinely, demand recompense for his neutrality to the tune of fifty kopecks, or even a rouble.

Oh, forget the vodka. That's depressing. It's better to tell you more about the kebabs: they exuded a fine, earthy, meaty aroma, they were crisp on the teeth and melted on the tongues of the diners, they were the perfect incarnation of cooked pork. And many was the time and not for nothing did the inebriated admirers of the pork kebabs burst into applause and call for the manager and wondrous creator Svidersky to come and greet, talk and drink with the working people, who spent their leisure time in the little restaurant and had many a time thus found a practical solution to the acute problem of how to spend one's leisure time, but they never succeeded in their endeavour, because Svidersky lived only for his work somewhere at the back of the restaurant, amid the cooking pots, hotplates, saucepans, pressure cookers and chests, in the office amid the rustling invoices, the accounts and the bills, amid the award certificates, the safes, the red pennant, signifying first prize for achievement.

You could see everyone there – the waitresses Nelly, Rimma, Shura, Tanya and Natasha, Esfir Ivanovna who worked behind the counter, the shift-working doormen who were friends, Kempendyaev and Kozlov, you even saw the cooks now and again, but the manager – never.

Well, all right then.

All those who visited the restaurant knew that the establishment was quiet, nice, efficient and well ventilated, but what kind of misfortune it was that bedevilled this orderly, amicable, collective of workers which ran like clockwork? – that was something that no one saw, no one knew about; "know about"? – they couldn't even have started to guess.

And the hub of the misfortune was that the successive carters who did the deliveries for the "Poddelkovo" had always been a choice bunch: first-rate piss heads, foul-mouthed individuals, thieves, womanizers – each in his own way, but none the less to a man, first-rate examples of the scum-bags of humanity.

The behaviour of the worst of them, a certain Ordasov, repeated and supplemented the behaviour of his ten predecessors: his horse turned green and use to sway from side to side through being starved and beaten. Ordasov would pop into the kitchen, he just had to have the first skewer with a kebab on it, he'd demand a bottle of beer, then a second, then a third, and if the washer-up or some other woman had to go out into the yard for the call of nature or to do a job, then it was a certainty that Ordasov would start groping her and making explicit suggestions, which featured the loft over the restaurant stables and the hay which was kept there, and the softness of this hay. And if for some reason or other his attempts at seduction were not crowned with success, then Ordasov would immediately unleash a flood of obscenities and name-calling – in particular he coined the humiliating term, in the circumstances, "spoon-washer" for the working woman.

Although one or two people might not like it, the work collective evidently breathed a sigh of relief, when it discovered that the carter Ordasov had eventually sold someone on the side a slab of butter, and drunk the money away, for which he was taken into custody by agents of the anti-corruption squad, he broke down at his interrogation, confessed to everything and was soon dispatched to the appropriate place.

So, one fine, bright morning, when nature was just awakening, when the little birds had just started to chirrup, when dew still moistened the asphalt on the roads, when they were just putting together the ingredients for the soup in the restaurant, and the sauce chef Vitya was just doing up the yellow buttons on his white coat, when everything was just getting going – everyone noticed the sudden arrival in the yard of a young man they had never seen before, in appearance, tall and morose, a stranger. His dress was odd, but not excessively so: Moscow-made jeans, a fine pair of hiking boots costing six roubles, a grey terylene shirt, the right sleeve of which was unfastened.

Everyone was surprised at the arrival of the morose stranger, and the young man, ferreting around in his trousers, pulled out a whip, walked over, tapped with the whip handle on the window and said: "Aggy? Uhu?"

Everyone froze on seeing this strange behaviour and hearing these strange words, but the young man described a circle round the yard, then opened the heavy stable door with a kick of his fine boot, led out the horse called Rogneda, trundled out the two-axle cart – and in the twinkling of an eye the collar was round the horse's neck, the cart was set behind Rogneda – and in a word, the restaurant's delivery department was on the move.

"He's the new carter!" shouted the sauce chef, and all the employees came helter-skelter out into the yard.

And green was the grass, yellow were the dandelions, and you could even see warm vapour rising clear as day from Rogneda's dung, and there was the new carter introducing himself to his new workmates.

"I'm Anikustsiya, and I'm your new delibbery man, I'll delibber on the 'orsh, I'll 'go gee-gee' on the 'orsh. Aggy?"

"Uh-uh," they replied with tender emotion.

And this is what the new carter did next.

He pulled down the collar of his shirt on his right shoulder, so that the sleeve that was unfastened covered his right fist completely, he stamped his foot on the ground and broke into song: "The locomotive goesh its way, but who knows where it goin' to!" And he shouted: "Women! Puff, puff, puff!"

"Oh, the poor cripple, that's what we've got, a poor cripple," was how the compassionate waitresses interpreted this scene.

"Well then, Anikusha, it's time to do some work," said a kind, yet at the same time, stern voice resonantly.

There was a whirlwind of activity, all hustle and bustle, and everyone made a beeline for the cooking pots and the pressure cookers, the kebab skewers, the frying pans and the potato peelers, the graters, the syphons, the sauce boats, the meat cleavers, the colanders – because Oleg Alexandrovich Svidersky, the comrade manager himself, had come out onto the reinforced concrete rear porch of the restaurant.

And with well-judged steps, he made his way over to Anikusha, and said the following words to him: "Anikusha! Work well and don't steal anything and you'll live well."

That's what Svidersky said, and Anikusha lowered his head, looked sad, but cheered up a second later, piled a lot of empty boxes onto the cart until it was full and ceremoniously rode out of the green gates to do his work.

This was when the restaurant finally attained its real heyday, when the work collective's battle brigade was brought up to full strength by a top-quality new cartridge with a good percussion cap and a sufficient quantity of gunpowder, with a bullet head, though small, made of lead.

And even the kebabs started to taste better, more perfect, and the circle of their admirers widened unremittingly, and in a short time the restaurant at Poddelkovo Station was constantly packed out with customers.

There were physicists from the atomic station. They were serious-looking, bespectacled, they wore nylon shirts and short ties, yet in essence they were very unassuming lads: they told jokes, and one of them, no doubt one of the younger ones, a real whizz kid, sang a rather dubious song, though he had wonderful eyes which expressed clear confidence in our ideals, he was just a young lad, just hadn't settled down yet . . . They ate . . . praised the food . . .

There were macro-biologists, who for some reason, didn't stink of animals at all, even though, various types of turtles had close relations with the scientists and were much loved by them. They were good people, but somehow awfully soft and kind, all of them just like one lady from their company, who spoke these words: "I can't believe it. No, just imagine. Comrades! Vitya, Alik – just can't believe it – in the back of beyond like this, eighty kilometres from Moscow, and cooking like this, and service like this! You know that I'm Russian, but I came to Moscow from Baku and I used to eat kebabs down there. And then look at this: this reminds me of my sunny home town, and it brings tears to my eyes and just makes me open out like a lily in the rain."

And her friends – Vitya, Alik with the bald bonce, Emmochka and Emmanuel – clinked their glasses of state liquor store Moskovskaya vodka loudly, and ate and praised the food.

There were also visiting students from Moscow, representatives of the new generation of fathers and children. They dropped in, tasted the food, gasped, ate it up and praised it, and tuned their electric guitars, and they themselves were clean shaven but had long hair and wore flared trousers and Japanese sweaters. Yes, and when they started playing "big beat" in harmony, then everyone recognized that there was no way they should have been condemned for it, and that it was not just the trousers and the hairstyles that determined the quality of a man, as the poet Evtushenko had once said. And that jazz was also a very good thing, for it didn't do anyone any harm, and we also know about classical music too and have a lot of time for it, but only as it adapts to the modern stuff; no, no, don't you start thinking that the categories are being turned inside out, no, it's not like that at all, after all, we're living in an era of innovation, the era of maths and physics faculties, the era of maths and physics schools, the age of the physicist who understands everything and yet can still see the irony of a situation. That was roughly what the visiting students had been trying to do all along when they played, it was explained afterwards – trainee geologists and ordinary people came in droves to their performances, and they all ate and praised the food.

And even the chairman of the CPC, Lysov, who was a sick man, the inventor of a perpetual-motion engine, allowed out one warm summer evening by his sympathetic doctor to go for a walk on his own, slipped into the restaurant and, at a table in the corner, with a mirror on the left and a reproduction of Surikov's *The Noblewoman Morozova* on the right, was chatting to a physicist he'd only just met about the history and future prospects of his invention. Lysov himself was rather short of stature with a widow's peak and had the drowsy-looking face of an idiot. He hadn't always been in the psychiatric hospital, he ended up there because of a half-length fur coat. He'd stolen the fur coat at the bazaar. He would have worked till his dying day, developing his perpetual-motion engine and elaborating a philosophical proof of its existence, because from the word go he had understood life all around him as a perpetual-motion engine in operation. But the only thing he didn't know was what kind of an engine his perpetual-motion engine was going to have. He worked on a prototype of it after work – one must say that Lysov was a good craftsman, if nothing else – but then he swiped this half-length fur coat from the bazaar and was given a few months inside, and there he started shouting his head off and talking all sorts of rubbish; in particular, he told everyone about his perpetual motion engine, even the administration, and so he was given a pardon over the fur coat, but sent away for compulsory medical treatment, and that was when Lysov made a career for himself, the crowning glory of which was the congenial and honorary post of chairman of the Community Patients' Council.

The madman and the physicist were having a heated argument, and the physicist was saying to the sick Lysov: "Listen here, mate, you're a clever man, mate, and you know that the idea of perpetual motion is a lot of nonsense and better minds than yours have come a cropper over that one, and you can't but help realize how pathetic you are in the face of world science."

Chairman Lysov burst into tears, put his arms round the physicist and finally made a clean breast of it, saying that he might succeed in building the engine, that was true, but that he did not believe in its long-term existence and operation for the simple reason that its components and transmission belts would wear out and you would have to fit new ones, and consequently the engine, even if it got going, could not be perpetual. As they talked the cruelty and harshness of science made them weep, but they ate and they praised the food.

Now while all this was in full swing, Anikusha the carter would sit in the kitchen and with a mouth wide open with profound thoughts, explain to all those who were interested, how much he loved cats and dogs and fish and birds, and also flowers and grass. When there was nothing for him to do at work, he would rush around the establishment, jumping, bounding, bleating, and even slipping into places that were quite off limits – the storeroom, the cold store, but forget the cold store: he even slipped into the holiest of holies, the manager's office, and there too he jumped and bounded about, even if Svidersky had visitors – and it was strange, but Oleg Alexandrovich never really lost his temper with his not over-blessed employee, in fact he praised him and said kind things to him. That's how one little man can help society understand another man, a big man. Everyone suddenly saw that that dear, kind, weary man, no longer young, Oleg Alexandrovich Svidersky, the manager of the restaurant, who had seen a lot in his life-time, and had somewhere, somehow suffered for it, why he had become wise and aloof, and yet had remained his own man, dear and not without talent.

And Anikusha was diligent, unlike the previous carters: he worked from morning to midnight, and sometimes he even installed himself overnight in the stables, and he didn't play about, he didn't drink, he didn't steal, he didn't play cards, he didn't spill pepper on the hotplate when it was on, he didn't skulk in corners, so that everyone thought it odd to see such good behaviour in a run-of-the-mill idiot.

And there was something else. Several people noticed that sometimes Anikusha emitted a strange light. Not the kind of light, let's say, that Christ or the saints emitted – constant and emanating from the head. No, on the contrary, it was intermittent. And it didn't come from his head at all, but from his navel. There it was – just a flash. Yes, yes. Sort of intermittent and coming from somewhere down below, well, from the navel or somewhere. But they didn't pay attention to this phenomenon: a lot of incomprehensible things can happen to those who are blessed, and you can see all sorts of things if you spend all day slaving over a hot stove, turning sodding skewers of pork kebabs and doing a mountain of washing up – it's hard work in the catering trade, I don't care what you say, and someone who's tired can start seeing all sorts of things.

But how astounded everyone was when the whole business was over and there turned out to be a very simple explanation.

A car arrived. The restaurant was sealed up, and Svidersky, a whiter shade of pale, cast a farewell glance over his brainchild and strode into the impenetrable darkness of the Black Maria, where someone with a pistol at his hip was waiting for him. And the Maria conveyed the manager through the sleeping streets straight into solitary confinement, where he was shaved, covered in prison garb and uncovered: citizen Svidersky, born 1915, nationality Russian, no dependents, single, not having fought in the war, previous police record – he was uncovered as the perpetrator of a terrible and loathsome crime, to wit: it turned out that the kebabs which were famed throughout the district were not pork kebabs at all, but were made of ordinary dog flesh. Beetles, Tobies, Palms, Rexes, Jacks, Typhoons, Squirrels – Oleg Alexandrovich Svidersky had taken the lot and reconstituted them as processed meat.

Now, you just imagine it for yourself, dear reader! – such degeneracy and such loathsomeness that in this great year of the existence of Soviet power, this son of a bitch, this grey-haired scoundrel conspiring with similar disgusting, loathsome persons, having wormed their way into a nice little restaurant outside Moscow, had been tearing the hides off of all those little Tobies and – urrgh – chopped up the meat, the dog flesh, the filthy stuff, and cooked it, the scoundrel!

And another disgrace was that our gourmets, lovers of fine gustatory sensations, had been taken in. "Kebabs are just kebabs all the world over", they seemed to be saying, and they'd stuff themselves full of cat meat, given half a chance. And the connoisseurs too, they couldn't tell pork from dog.

By way of comfort to the deceived public, I was on the point of relating a story which an old woman in the bazaar in the city of K. had told me about herself, how she used the fat from her puppy Kutka to cure five people of coughspit-consumption, and that they generally use dog fat to treat tuberculosis, but when I saw the treacherous fat mugs of the witnesses in the courtroom, I abandoned the idea completely, afraid that they would ridicule me or perhaps even beat me up, being such strong people, who had been reared on dog-meat kebabs and were afraid of nothing.

And Anikusha disappeared as well. At first people thought that he was the chief kebabman's right hand, but then they realized that, actually, he had stayed Svidersky's hand and got his paw on his throat, squeezing him in a policeman's grip of steel. For of course, Anikusha turned out to be none other than Detective Sergeant Vzglyadov of the police. He caught him, exposed him and even photographed individual dark deeds on microfilm and with a microflash. That was where that mysterious light kept coming from, ah you dopes and swindlers, night blindness.

The trial, held in the old court house, in an old street with an old prosecutor in charge, of course, reverberated. Half of Poddelkovo came flocking to it, as well as people from other towns, kebab lovers.

Svidersky repented and cried his bloody eyes out, but not a glimmer of compassion flickered in the eyes of the public. Someone demanded that he be given the ultimate punishment – death by firing squad, and although it was clear from the outset that no one was going to get the six o'clock walk on account of some dogs, everyone was very keen on the idea.

Even his lawyer just kept picking his teeth with the sharpened end of a match for some reason. No one knew what he was trying to say by this, but if you thought about it carefully you could guess – I'm defending you, Svidersky, as best I can, but only because it's my job, this is my sad duty on this earth, to defend riffraff like you from the punishment they deserve.

And Svidersky received a sentence that was neither too heavy nor too light: he got exactly what he should have got according to the law of the land, and the malicious inventor was spirited out of court to the accompaniment of commotion all round, having sown mighty seeds of discord and scepticism in the carefree hearts of inoffensive gourmets.

After a time, while this was still going on, the restaurant was reopened and renovated by a brawny body of workmen. They got a new waiter called Borya, born in 1945, excused military service, loved telling the customers about how three years in a row he had failed the entrance exams to the S. Ordzhonikidze Geological-Prospecting Institute in Moscow, a new despatch clerk, a new cashier, a new carter, and of course, they wouldn't have got by without a new manager – Zorykin by name. Unlike his predecessor, he was jolly, stentorian, and, with his beer gut sticking out, he loved sitting down with the customers, regaling the respected recipients with stories from his own, Zorykin's, life.

But under his management the kebabs went right downhill. They became too grey, too brown, too lacklustre, and much smaller, as if they were cringing in shame at their external appearance. And you didn't feel like even putting one of them in your mouth, so what were you supposed to do with them, one asks? – Svidersky had taught people that they couldn't get through the day without a kebab.

And soon this manager was also nicked, which sounds very strange, especially when you consider that a bomb never falls in the same place twice. By chance it came to light that he was skimping four grams on every portion of meat and pocketing the difference, and had amassed a fortune running into many thousands on the proceeds. True, when they searched his premises they only found two thousand, but the possibility can't be excluded that he'd stashed the other thousands somewhere else: maybe he had simply gone and buried them in the garden under an apple tree, and he'd come back later, all the fitter from the physical labour he'd had to perform, an able-bodied man, and say, I'll just go and dig up some worms for fishing bait, and he'd dig up the booty and begin a new life in seclusion, saving his soul with reflections on the imperfections of human nature – of greed and stupidity. Another fine fellow!

And then a new summer came. 1967. Greenery. Lilac engulfed the town. The flowering of the lilac was a sea – only the roofs of the houses sticking out, while the people, like mysterious sea creatures, darted about in the murky cool of the streets below.

The windows were open wide in the Poddelkovo restaurant at the Poddelkovo Station on the Moscow railway, they were open wide and covered with cheese cloth to keep the flies out.

The fans were humming, people were sitting, the fans were humming, and to the accompaniment of the humming the people had been arguing endlessly for months as to who had been the worse of the two managers. Usually it was the railway coupler Mikheev, a regular customer at the restaurant since receiving a good sum in injury benefit for a leg he had broken at work, who was on Svidersky's side. Now his voice rose above the noise of the air conditioning and overlay the buzz of converstaion in the restaurant: "I reckon that Svidersky, even though he was a real shit, a bastard, Lord forgive me, a dog-breeder, he still provided decent meals – and there was a lot of it, and it was tasty, and ain't it all the same to you whether it's dog or pig?"

"Zorykin was also a rat, a thief to tell you straight, but when all's said and done, he did serve up proper meat, even though there wasn't much of it."

"Well, a lot you know . . ."

"Yeah, well . . ."

And no one knows how this absurd argument would have finally ended, since at exactly that moment the fans ceased their humming, for the simple reason that they had been turned off to save a little bit of electricity, seeing as the temperature in the room had gone down, and from a loudspeaker there boomed the sounds of a new song which had only just got into the charts, now being performed to the accompaniment of various jolly-electric instruments by the class of '67, wearing flared trousers and collarless jackets, the sounds of the song, which in the graphic words of the radio announcer, had become the hit of the season, symbol number one of our bright summer, a summer of young people, the summer of '67:

*Come back. I've been so long without you!*
*Come back. Without your love I'm so blue.*

Etc. etc. It was about the Sirocco wind. Anyway, you know the song, of course. And if – by some miracle – you had been in that little restaurant at Poddelkovo Station, you would have promptly joined in with the unseen radio singers, as did all the debaters, having promptly forgotten all about the criminal managers, those two scoundrels of '67, or then again, maybe the words of the song referred to them. They were all singing in earnest, stretching their necks and pulling in their stomachs, singing obliviously, neither eating nor occupied with anything other than the singing, and here we shall bid a sad farewell to this jolly restaurant and distance ourselves from it in order to examine the amazing things that go on in other corners of our Homeland, like for example in Yakutia, in the north, where an amazing story took place: a man, a stoker in a brewery, fell into a beer vat and he lay there for the best part of a month, until his body was spotted, and as soon as the local population got to hear about it, not only did they not drink beer for a whole month, but they didn't drink vodka either, fearing that they would encounter the deceased in solution and thus be party to cannibalism. Now isn't that amazing!

I ought to write a story about that as well, but I'm afraid it would be difficult to get it published.

# Emanation

I'm not ashamed to state the fact until I'm blue in the face: our Siberian golden autumn is splendid, when the leaves rustle underfoot, and a damp blue haze wafts off the Enisei, and the swans, calling out, fly off to Egypt, and the sun wanes, eases off towards evening, and the poplar trembles gently in the noonday heat haze, and a lump comes to your throat when you see the lovely little red tram crawling over the grey concrete bridge against the vast background of the bright, ochre-speckled blue, green and violet autumn taiga.

And look, there's a girl. The girl has got out of the lovely little red tram, and she is slowly making her way down to the Enisei, absent-mindedly taking the occasional kick at the odd little pebble she comes across with the toe of her suede shoe. Her name is Anya. She is twenty-six years old. She is studying at the local teachers' training college and she lives with her parents.

And against the background of all this charming landscape as described above, Anya came out onto the steep bank and started to make her way down to the gentle waves, whose idle lapping disturbed not even the huge works of the dredger which was moored in the channel and whose thick pipes stretched way over to the right bank of the river with the aim of creating a shingle embankment for the expanding combine factory. The dredger was silent. Anya came out onto that native bank of hers and made for the gentle waves.

And sitting there on the pebbles, unable to be seen from above, was her future husband, Vasya. Wearing a scruffy black sweater, ordinary trousers and long hair, he screwed up his eyes and struck up on his guitar:

*Hear me, my darling . . .*

Anya shuddered when she saw this lad she didn't know and heard these words, but she didn't give away that she was embarrassed and could hear them. And she didn't change direction, just in case Vasya started thinking about her something along the same lines as she might be thinking about him.

She went gingerly up to the very edge of the Enisei, stood there for a moment, her lips scarcely moving, and then bowed deeply and Vasya heard a quiet: "Hello, Water . . ."

And Vasya saw her long, neat legs in their nice white stockings, and the edge of her white panties as her mini-skirt rode up. And Vasya gasped and promptly made a thorough visual assessment of her: a scrawny little girl with corkscrew ringlets, a quiet girl, as was to be seen.

He felt a flood of extraordinary inspiration come over him and once again plucked at the guitar strings:

*Hear me, my darling . . .*

Then an icy shiver ran down the girl's back, she straightened up, and without a word moved to one side, sat down on a boulder and ostentatiously opened an interesting little book.

"Da-arl-ing . . ."

Anya turned a page.

"Excuse me, miss, but what are you reading that's so interesting. Couldn't I read with you as well?" asked Vasya, cheekily, as it were, though he had never been one to put himself about particularly.

Anya heard nothing.

"Are you deaf or something, miss?" asked her emboldened future husband, coming over to her.

And so it was he came over, gauche, embarrassed, trying to smile, holding the beautiful guitar in his outstretched hand. That was how Anya saw him, as she resentfully turned her neat little head.

"Darling . . ." said Vasya with a smile.

And at that point the girl slammed the book shut and jumped up angrily. She tensed herself, coiled ready to . . .

And at that point the engines of the hitherto silent dredger started up. Rattling and roaring, terrible rattling and roaring issued from the dredger, unseen stones clanked and crashed through its thick pipes.

The girl was waving her arms, the girl was shouting something angrily, but Vasya Feskov, quite taken aback, could not hear her. Her face was terribly contorted and had turned crimson, she was scything the air with her little fist.

And all of a sudden the awful noise ceased, in the ensuing silence Anya was unable to utter a single word. She was panting for breath, she was glaring furiously, she suddenly hissed: "Fool!"

And she dealt Vasya a resounding slap.

Vasya went white, stepped back and clenched his teeth.

And she suddenly burst into tears. At first she sobbed and howled, and then it started: "Ow-ow-ow . . ." she gulped, "Ow-ow-ow . . ." Her little bird-like body, her scrawny little neck, twitched.

"Miss, what's the matter? What's the matter?" asked the good Vasya, forlornly.

And she suddenly weakened, stuck her face in his sweater, and still sobbing plaintively, mumbled: "How corny everybody is, how – corny everybody is, why is everybody so corny?"

"What are you saying, darling, what are you saying?" said Vasya, at a complete loss, and with no idea of what he was doing, clumsily put his arm round her and started to stroke her dry, fragrant hair.

And the girl calmed down, without realizing what she was doing, lay her head on his shoulder, her eyes closed. Then she suddenly came to her senses, looked at Vasya in hatred, recoiled and ran. He dashed off after her. She was panting, and he was panting. They were both panting.

That's how the future married couple got to know each other. And well, soon after this romantic event, they were married, entering a state of legal matrimony by reason of their suddenly kindled love, which love they formalized in a department of the Central District Registry Office. Anya's happy parents congratulated them, although they were a bit apprehensive that Vasya would turn out to be a drinker, and Vasya's old aunt, with whom, being a complete orphan, he had stayed all his life, even burst into tears. Vasya's friends assumed a deferential, polite air. Anya's fellow students whispered all the more among themselves.

Their life together began so happily and felicitously. You'd just love it, if you could take a look at them, at those twenty-six-year-old love-birds. You just wouldn't recognize the old, ecstatic Anya now, singing slushy songs, as she vacuumed their carpets, polished for the hundredth time the varnished parquet floor of that one-room co-operative flat, which Anya's provident parents had given them, having wisely reckoned that sooner or later even she, their beloved little daughter, would get married, and not stay a spinster until the end of time. By this time Anya had finished at the teachers' training college and was working as a music teacher at three kindergartens simultaneously, doing one and a half full time jobs. She worried so much about Vasya, she worried so much about him, that at times he even felt sort of awkward about it.

"Vasya, just what do you think you're up to?" Anya would suddenly ask in horror.

"What? What?" Vasya would reply in fright.

"Why are you wearing those old trousers?"

"I like them."

"Take them off right away. They're creased."

"So what if they're creased, what the hell . . ."

"Don't 'hell' me, in the old days you could go around looking scruffy and dirty. But now you're a married man. You go out with me. Everyone will say that I'm not looking after you."

"Couldn't care less what they say," Vasya would snap back, but he still went and changed his trousers, rightly considering that it was only a triviality and it wasn't worth having a quarrel over trivialities.

He himself, so it seemed to him, hadn't changed at all. Just as before, he was cheerful, even-tempered, hale and hearty. True, he had had to part company with the institute for a time – Anya was sitting her state examinations, they needed money, and so Vasya had gone to work as a technician in a mineral laboratory. And somehow or other, imperceptibly, there he stayed. He played the guitar a bit now and then, occasionally met his friends, who were as yet unmarried.

"Everything's all right, mates," he'd say. "I think I've done the right thing. I did it myself, and I've done the right thing. And anyway, let me tell you something – you've got to have soup in the house."

"You can get soup in the canteen," his friends objected.

"That's not the point, that's not the point . . ." Vasya would say with a laugh. "You can get soup in the canteen, but there's no . . . emanation. Do you understand? Emanation. When everything's intense and everything is giving off a magical glow, an invisible glow of happiness."

At this point one of his jocular friends would feel Vasya's forehead anxiously, at which Vasya would be the first to laugh.

But, well, if one were to make an honest confession, some sort of little worm had begun, had begun to gnaw at him. Because everything was sort of going along normally, yet not quite right, not quite right . . . On the one hand, it's probably really a good thing when a woman is looking after you, asking you not to go out on the town and not to go spending the night in the house of your fun-loving pals. When she irons your shirts and estimates whether your monthly money, on which you survive without any fuss or bother, is enough to last until payday. Of course that's a good thing, otherwise how would it be? Otherwise you'd be lost, you'd go right downhill, you'd be worthless, you'd perish irrevocably.

And as he was, or part of him was, a rational man, Vasya understood this with his intellect, but his whole being, despite the excellence of the logic, rebelled against such tutelage, which he found so inexplicably humiliating. Was he short of breath or something? He knew that there even existed a technical term for what was happening to him: "hen-pecked", but why was it happening so quickly? Why so quickly?

And soon the young husband began to conduct himself, to put it delicately, not altogether correctly. He started to break things, to misbehave, to smile unpleasantly. And he was especially annoyed by the fact that Anya wasn't especially surprised by such a change in his conduct. As if she had long been prepared for it. Imperturbably and calmly she insisted on what she said, and when Vasya used foul language, she locked herself, for want of anywhere else, in the bathroom and there she quietly read, by this very action reducing him to a state of blind rage.

This was how their humdrum days passed – in petty hostility and quarrels, just as their nights passed in ardent love-making.

These shocks and abrupt transitions caused Vasya to start cracking up completely. He was often rude, and on one occasion, in a rage, he even raised his fist to Anya.

This is how it happened. In his early youth Vasya used to dabble in poetry. His poems weren't up to much. Vasya came to realize this and soon abandoned his prosodic pursuits. But he had a huge storehouse of a book in which he noted any thoughts, phrases and musings that he had personally thought up himself. On life and death, love and truth, musings to the effect that God doesn't exist, but it would be better if he did. Vasya had no purpose in mind in committing these notes to paper. Actually, perhaps I'm not altogether correct on this point. There were times when it seemed to him that it was a framework, a foundation on which one day he would construct a good, honest, intelligent book, not a "storehouse" book, but an eternal one, he would construct it and by that very act justify his existence in the world. For he, Vasily Feskov, wasn't born on earth just to eat, sleep, go to work, kiss Anya like this. Even though eating was nice, sleeping was nice, and kissing Anya was lovely.

And here's something else that's interesting. For some reason he never showed his notes to Anya. And she herself didn't display any particular curiosity whenever he pulled the book out of the old suitcase tucked away on the storage shelf, wrinkled his brow and wrote down in it in his small, rounded script his current, as he put it, "sensible idea".

On that black day, when it all happened, Vasya came home from work, had a bite to eat, and decided to make a note in his book of the yells of a distraught man he'd seen on the bus. This man had been shouting that he'd just come from the morgue where his dear friend was lying, lying lifeless, because he had fallen under a train. "Sashka, Sashka!" shouted the man. "What have you done, Sashka! After all, you weren't drunk, you were on your way to work, Sashka!"

These absurd cries were what Vasya wanted to make a note of. But he couldn't find his book on the storage shelf. He hunted through one suitcase, then another, but the book was nowhere to be seen.

"Anya, you haven't by chance seen that book I had, have you? It's got 'Storehouse' written on it, a green, thick book?" he asked.

"Yes, I have," answered Anya, sitting in front of the television with her sewing on her lap.

"Where is it then?"

"It's in the rubbish chute," Anya answered calmly.

"What did you say? Are you joking?" said Vasya, turning white.

"No, I'm not joking," answered Anya amiably, "I'm not joking at all."

Vasya ran out on to the landing and opened the rubbish chute. There, stuck to its damp inside, was a scrap of paper.

". . . ife is given to man by chance. Through chanc . . .
. . . coincidence I appeared in this world. So what then is a ma . . .
. . . cowardly clinging on to it. The world! Pulling and tormen . . ."

"What did you do that for?" said Vasya, bounding back into the room.

"Ooh, what an angry little hubby I've got," said Anya with a smile.

"I'm asking you a question!"

"And I'm answering you! I came across it by accident. And I read it by accident. And do you know what, I'll tell you something, I've never seen such corniness, filth, obscenity and tastelessness in all my life . . ."

"And what business is it of yours?" said Vasya, choking with anger.

"Would you be a bit more polite, please, a bit more polite. I won't argue with you that, when all's said and done, maybe it's none of my business that you write nasty things, even about me. But you ought to at least think a bit! WHAT are you writing? Whether you like it or not, you're a family man now!"

That was when Vasya raised his fist to her.

"Oh, you silly cow!" he shouted.

But Anya was looking at him in her usual calm fashion, somehow, I would even say, in a fashion radiant, carefree, indifferent.

"If you ever, even once, hit me, I'll leave you on the spot."

"Oh, you silly cow!" shouted Vasya. "Why are you always trying to spite me? Are you cleverer than me or something?"

"Calm down!" she hurled at him mockingly, and turned away to go off into the bathroom, as was her custom.

"Oh, hell!" howled Vasya, and pushing her aside, rushed in there first and shut the door on the hook.

With trembling hands he tore the belt out of his trousers and then stopped, quite at a loss, because he had never once in his life before hanged himself, and he didn't know how to do it.

He went over to the mirror and tried on the belt like a tie. An almost unfamiliar, enraged face looked out of the mirror at him.

"Open the door! Open the door! Vasily, open the door this minute!" shouted Anya pounding impotently on the door, sensing somehow instinctively that this time things were really bad. "Open the door, open the door! Dear, good, darling Vasya, come on, open the door, open the door, open the door!"

"Well, what are you shouting your head off for?" asked Vasya rudely, throwing the door open violently.

"Vasya, I didn't get a chance to tell you. We're, we're going to have a baby! . . ."

And Anya burst into unrestrained sobs.

"Come on, why are you crying?" said Vasya more softly, involuntarily putting his arms round her.

"No, tell me, are you happy, tell me are you happy, are you?" she kept repeating, throwing back her tear-stained face.

"Yes, I'm happy, I am," said Vasya wrinkling his brow.

And about seventy years before him the writer Lev Tolstoy said that all happy families are alike. Good Lord, was the wise old man of Yasnaya Polyana really right in fact?

# Ruin

Once upon a time there lived near Uar Station on the East Siberian railway a quiet little girl. Her daddy turned out to be a right son of a bitch and one day he cleared off, no one knows where, while her mummy was always ill, always ill, going down with something. Once she even went on a package trip to the Lake Shira health resort. She was ill, always ill, and then she died quietly and unnoticed, humbly and painlessly.

And the little girl buried her mummy and put up a cross with a photograph on it. Mummy looked out from the photograph like a living person. The little girl grieved a bit, bade farewell to a surviving distant aunt and went away to the town.

And there she was walking along a street when she suddenly saw a scrap of paper stuck crookedly onto a post:

RUME TOO LET. SUTE YOUNG GERL. IN POKROVKA

She set off to the address, which turned out to be that of a bent-backed, crafty old crone. The woman took three months rent off her in advance, ordered her not to bring anyone back, not to come home late or "start boozing and carrying on with men in her house". That very first evening she herself got drunk on Solntsedar wine and went off into her vegetable patch to have a row with her neighbour. The neighbour hit her on the head with a sunflower. The old woman yelled out, hitched up her skirts and showed her her arse. There's scarcely a person alive that can put up with an insult like that – the neighbour went for her tooth and nail, the local copper came along, and took statements.

At first the girl wanted to go to the business studies college, but as it turned out, there were no places vacant that year. So then she got fixed up at the post office and started delivering letters, parcels and postal orders.

She didn't have any girlfriends. One day she went to a dance at the Polytechnic, and there a tall, longhaired guy asked her to dance. He looked like one of the Balladeers folk group who sing, to the accompaniment of electrical instruments, on records of that name, in sweet, ringing tones. His name was Vovik. He saw her home as far as her gate, stood there, had a smoke, and got his hand in her bra, received a rebuff, but came back again the next day, and the old woman said to her: "Don't you get mixed up with that good-for-nothing. I can see by his mug that he'll be the ruin of you."

"Oh, I'm not thinking of anything like that," said the girl.

"You think whatever you like, but if you get mixed up with him, he'll be the ruin of you," insisted the old woman.

But the girl didn't believe her. They went out to dances together, to the cinema, twice he took her back to his place, where he came on really strong. But the first time, his dad interrupted them. He turned the key in the lock and shouted cheerfully into the depths of the huge flat: 'Ullo! People! The breadwinner's just come back from a meeting, hungry as forty thousand wolves!"

And the second time the girl herself tore herself away from him at the last second and ran off. Vovik stayed lying there in a foul temper, calling after her all the names he could lay his tongue to. But the next day they met again.

And well, soon she, somehow, without even noticing it much herself, sort of permitted what she shouldn't have, and a month later she was sick in the yard, in the presence of the old woman.

"I stuffed myself with liver sausage," said the girl.

And the old woman looked at her intently.

"Just so long as that liver sausage don't start giving you cravings for pickles and slaked lime," said the old woman.

And the girl didn't understand at first what she'd said that for, but she did later on.

Then she went to see to Vovik, and Vovik's mum opened the door to her.

"Hello," said the girl, "Can I see Volodya?"

"Volodya's not in," replied Volodya's mum with a hostile glare.

"Where can I find him, then?" asked the girl.

"No point in trying," replied his mummy. "You girls are always coming here, always. I'm fed up with it. If he needs to, he'll find you himself. No point in distracting him from his studies. He's got exams coming up!"

And she slammed the door. And the girl went over to the wall, scratched at the plaster and waited. But Vovik didn't come. Other people came in the main entrance: wheeling prams, carrying parcels, bags and packages. They greeted each other, they laughed. But there was still no Vovik. The girl went home.

Still no Vovik. Once the girl saw him through a pane of glass. He was travelling on the rear platform of a tram and he was waving his arms, explaining something to his friends. He threw a vacant look her way, but in fact, in all probability, didn't notice the girl.

And she went to a public baths. She bought a ticket for thirty-five kopecks and went into a shower cubicle. She took out a small pocket mirror and started to look at her belly. Her belly, sure enough, was swollen. The girl turned on the tap. Water poured resonantly from the ceiling. The girl burst into tears.

And then one day she met Vovik's father. A tall man, even taller than Vovik himself, broad-shouldered, crewcut hair, dad stepped out of his car, swinging his briefcase.

"Hello there, poppet!" he said cheerfully. "Not coming in then? Or have you and that idiot Vovik had a row?"

"Oh, no," said the girl.

"And why are you so under the weather? Bags under your eyes?"

"I've got a bun in the oven," said the girl.

"What?" spluttered father. "Just what are you on about?"

And the girl told him the whole story there and then. And on the evening of the same day, dad conducted an extended conversation with his son.

"Well then, son, what are you intending to do about it?" he finally asked.

"Study, study and study still more," said Vovik with a shrug of his shoulders.

"And what's the girl going to do, you bastard?"

"I'll give her ten roubles and she can go and get it scraped out," replied Vovik and promptly received a straight right to the jaw.

Mother, who had been eavesdropping, burst into the room.

"Don't you dare beat a child, you fascist!" she shouted, "He's too young to get married. And that female is an adult. She knew what she was about. You didn't promise to marry her, did you, Vovik?"

"Of course not," said Vovik gloomily, sucking at the blood oozing from his mouth.

"I'm not going to allow my son to get married to the first country girl he comes across . . ."

"You will," mumbled father unpleasantly. "You will! Vovik is going to ask your permission, and you are going to say yes. That's right, isn't it, Vovik. Are you going to ask?"

"Look, what do I need her for, Dad? I've still got three years to do at school. So what do I need her for? And then again, who's to say that the baby's mine? Maybe it's not mine."

"You shit!" said Dad, looking in revulsion at his son. "You shit! Was it for the likes of you that I fought in the war, built buildings, froze, went hungry?"

"Oh, get stu . . ." said his wife.

"I won't!" exploded the builder. "He's fathered a child, let him get married. And let's hear no more about it. That's all there is to it! I'm not going to have my name dragged through the mud. Half the town knows me."

Unexpectedly Vovik piped up cheerfully: Oh well! S'pose I can get married. I don't give a damn! True, she isn't all that good looking. I've had more up-market goods."

Father smiled too.

"That doesn't matter," he said. "Don't you know the Eastern proverb? A beautiful wife is another man's wife."

"And if I get fed up with her, I can always pack her in," mused Vovik.

"I'll give you 'pack in'!" said Father, wagging a threatening finger at him.

Vovik's mother sobbed, and soon the young couple were standing in front of an official at a department of the Central District Registry Office.

The woman conducting the ceremony said: Hand in hand, for better or worse, for richer for poorer, you will go through life. So may your union be strong! May this new unit in our society, your young family, be strong! Comrades, hip hip!"

And the comrades said "hurray" and got in the car, which was all decked out in ribbons. Passers-by looked at the car. On the windscreen of the black Volga someone's solicitous hands had tied a huge celluloid doll.

Then came the wedding reception. There was everything you could think of on the tables. They even had red caviar. But they didn't have any relatives from the bride's side. Whereas from the groom's side many people made speeches and wished the young couple the most and best of all manner of things. The bride sat with eyes lowered.

"Let the young bride say something," someone shouted.

The bride stood up, cast a happy gaze over the table and all those present and said, addressing Vovik's parents: "Dear Mummy and Daddy! Please allow me to call you that now! It is no small service on your part that I have entered your house and become your daughter-in-law. Believe me when I say that I am very hardworking, and also that I will always value this and will never forget it."

And, unable to contain herself, she started to cry. The groom smiled condescendingly, but many of the others cried as well. Mummy cried, drying her eyes with a lace handkerchief. Daddy cried, chewing severely on his well trimmed moustache. Many cried! And they were crying, of course, from joy. From what else?

# Laughing and Smiling

In Minusinsk a long-haired young man, on a journey necessitated by the demands of artistic creativity, met a girl from his home town, of whom it was known that she was very advanced, and passed herself off as an *emancipé*.

They laughed. The girl was accompanied by her grandmother – a somewhat grey-haired, dryish Siberian old woman. Quietly, and with a little touch of good humour, they laughed at the clumsy old woman, they laughed at the latest comedy film they'd seen, they laughed at anything and everything, and then they all went to the bus station together. There grandmother made the sign of the cross over her little granddaughter, and gave the young man a chilly look. The young people boarded the bus and hit the road for Abakan – the young lady was intending to fly to Novosibirsk that evening, but as everyone knows, there are no planes from Minusinsk to Novosibirsk.

They stood in the square. By the Khakasia Hotel. They laughed. The young man pointed to the young lady's flat, little midriff, bared below her short, fashionable T-shirt.

What about the local population? Did they condemn or admire it?

The local population, by and large, reacted normally. Even too normally. Old ma Anfisa wanted to give the girl her staple dress.

Then the young man had a bright idea.

"I'll go to Novosibirsk as well. I'm like a lemon squeezed dry here. That's my lot! It's time for me to go home too!"

"Oh, you're an artist then, are you?" elaborated the young lady.

"Yes, I am . . . I am an artist," answered the young man

nonchalantly. "I'm a writer and an artist, and I'm Moby Dick, and I'm also the son of Lieutenant Schmidt. That's my lot! I'm flying home! Oh, the guys in the Art Design group will be pleased. Our piss artist has shown up, they'll say . . ."

"Do you drink a lot?" asked the young lady in surprise.

"No, only as required," said the young man, pulling a face. "By the way, maybe we could crack open a bottle of cognac, something on the cheap side, what do you say?"

"Great!" said the young lady, with a laugh. "But have we got time?"

"Oh, we've got time for everything," said the young man, mysteriously leaning over, and asking mysteriously, "and what's your position regarding sexual morality? Full sexual emancipation or only partial?"

At this the young lady gave the young man a fleeting smile and a fleeting wink.

And, delighted, the latter set about confiding such confidences as: I'm a soft man. I'm a weak-willed man. But I don't like spinning yarns, and I don't like secrets, and I don't like telling lies. Now you see, I've revealed my little plans to you honestly, and that's much better than if I was suddenly just sort of sitting around for hours and then just started suddenly groping you right out of the blue. Right?"

"Right," said the young lady, with a laugh.

"By the way, are you going to be long in Novosibirsk?"

"No, I'm going to take a break and join my parents in Mongolia for the holidays. They're top-flight geologists."

"Mongolia! Parents! Top-flight geologists! Pull the other one! How are they going to let you into the country? Though the Mongolians are our brothers, I suppose. How's it go – Hindi-Russky, bkhai-bkhai!"

"It's neither here nor there that they're our brothers," said the girl, turning serious. "For one thing, I'm getting an international passport. I went to my grandmother's just to pass the time quicker . . ."

And the time passed very quickly. One might say, the time flew past. Like an aeroplane. They got some cognac and some chocolate and they went upstairs – to the single room which the leading light in the art world was booked into.

"Get a load of the logo: 'The Khakasia Hotel – the Hilton of Abakan'," chuckled the young man.

He got a little dreamy, and the young lady got a bit drunk, and by this stage there wasn't much left in the bottle. The young man looked at his watch.

"Well, are you fit then?" he said. "Time for us to hit the sack, princess!"

"So soon? What for?" said the young lady, somewhat surprised.

"You know what for," said the young man, with a grin. "Now come on, or we'll miss the plane."

And he also gave her a wink. He, if I can be allowed to put it this way, returned her wink. He gave her a wink and slipped his hand smartly under her T-shirt. The young lady backed away.

"Don't even think it! Don't you dare!" she said, using the formal form of address.

"Why do you keep on addressing me so formally," said the young man, flaring up, and he seized the young lady by the elbows. "We agreed to use the familiar form."

"I can't do it so quickly," whispered the young lady. "Use the familiar form. I have to get used to it."

"Oh, stop playing around! What's all the fuss about! I explained everything to you, didn't I? And you agreed with it all. Pack in the airs and graces, woman. You can save your airs and graces for your schoolboy friends . . ."

"Don't even think it! Don't you dare!" the young lady kept repeating. "I should have told you the truth in the first place. I should, I should have, I'm just an innocent girl."

"Exactly," said the young man, brightly. "I was just a young girl . . . Look here, don't you think we've been fooling around enough? It's time to get down to business."

"But it's true, I'm only a girl. I'm a virgin."

And then the young man suddenly understood everything. He understood everything. He got up brusquely, walked over to the window brusquely and started drumming with his fingers on the pane brusquely.

"How come?" he grumbled. "What about Belyaev, the guy from the comedy theatre, didn't he ever come to your place?"

"Yes, but just like you now."

"You're spinning a yarn, aren't you?" asked the young man uncertainly.

"Why should I spin yarns. What's the point?" said the young lady, lowering her eyes.

"So where's this getting us?" said the young man, turning very nasty. "Haven't you got a head on your shoulders? Where's your sense of honour? And how am I to feel? I was all ready for it. I really was . . ."

And they looked into each other's eyes – an angry young man and a young lady wearing a T-shirt that was too short for her. The young lady shook her head and stared sadly. And he stared morosely.

"Well, I'll be going then," said the young lady.

"Say hello to Choibalsan for me," muttered the young man in response.

And the young lady left.The young man stood by the mirror.

"Laughing and smiling, and what was the point of it?" he complained to the mirror. "Took me in completely, led me right up the garden path . . ."

. . . Back in Minusinsk the young lady's grandmother scraped open her gate. Her dog, Beetle, dashed right under her feet. Grandmother lit the blue icon lamp and prayed and prayed to God! Then she had something to eat out of an enamel bowl and began looking out of the darkening window. Her lips moved, but she said nothing.

# The Drummer and the Drummer's Wife

Once upon a time there lived in the wide world a quiet woman who was disabled, and there also lived in the wide world together with her a lively drummer in a funeral orchestra.

At one time this woman had lived with her husband in the city of Karaganda in the Kazakh SSR and once she was travelling on a long-distance bus to work. Suddenly the engine in the bus conked out on a level crossing, and a train was too close.

The train hit the bus and produced a real mess and a lot of scrap iron. And the drummer's wife went flying out of the bus.

During the flight an iron-capped boot smashed her head open, and the bones stuck out, after which she started forever mumbling something, mumbling and mumbling, and also reading the same book over and over again. To be precise, it was Rasul Gamzatov's *Mountain Woman*, in which he describes the new relationships between people in the Republic of Daghestan and their struggle for women's equality.

She had bought this book in the hospital kiosk immediately after she had sustained her injuries. And she had never parted with it since.

After her accident a good many people turned their backs on the woman, and the first to do so was her own husband.

But the drummer played the drum all his life. He beat the drum in the war at the front, and after the war too he beat the drum. He drank heavily. He drank and drank and drank, until he started playing in a funeral orchestra, making music as they followed the coffins.

And then a good many people turned their backs on him too.

And then he and the woman met, and they started to live together in Zasukhina Street in temporarily built quarters.

Their home was draughty in winter, but the stove burnt brightly. And in the summer the bird cherry trees blossomed in their little garden, and they could get by all right. True, the drummer still drank and drank, and the woman still mumbled.

And the woman was beautiful – black-haired and slender.

And the drummer, apart from playing the drum, studied issues involving the durability of surrounding objects. He grieved deeply over the fact there were no durable things on earth. And that if there was a more or less durable object, then there was most certainly a more durable object which could destroy it.

"You know, if it wasn't like that, then your head wouldn't have been smashed by a metal-capped boot," he used to tell his wife.

And she would agree with him.

Always mindful of his unsuccessful search for the meaning of durability, the drummer drank more and more. Then one day, in utter despair, he turned on the holiest of holies: he climbed onto his drum and started to jump up and down on it. Testing it.

The woman was sitting on the bed.

She was sitting quietly on the bed and reading her favourite book. The wall clock was ticking quietly. The wooden walls of the temporary building were nicely whitewashed. There was a washbasin and a rubbish bin in the corner. There was a mat on the floor.

And the drummer kept jumping up and down, though he was small and plumpish. He kept jumping and jumping and eventually burst the drum, his bread and butter, his drink.

Then he got really upset, and began behaving badly. He started accusing his woman of ruining his life.

"If it wasn't for you, you fool, I'd be playing in the Bolshoi Theatre now. I could give you a good hiding."

The quiet woman was very frightened. Because they had lived together for a long time and he had never spoken to her like that before. She took her book and ran out into the street.

But it was night time outside, and the streetlamps weren't very bright, so you would run off only if you were in really desperate straits.

The drummer understood this, and he started to feel very ashamed. Then he went over to the standpipe. He was hairy. He stripped off, doused himself in cold water, went back home and cut open the duvet.

He rolled around in the feathers, and then set off to look for his woman.

He found her by the mound of earth that ran along the walls of the house. She was trembling with fear and peering in all directions into the darkness.

"Well, what are you afraid of, you fool? said the befeathered drummer. "Don't be afraid."

The drummer's woman said nothing.

"Don't be afraid, love," said the drummer, who was a lively individual. "I haven't smeared myself with tar, nor with honey. I poured water over myself, and you'll have no trouble washing me down. Do you want to?"

"Yes," answered the woman. She climbed out from under the mound, and started mumbling: "Yes, yes, yes."

And they went back into the house. The drummer put his arms round his wife. She heated up some water in a large clothes boiler. She poured the water into a butt and started to wash him.

And he sat in the butt and blew soap bubbles, to stop his wife from crying, and to make her laugh.

# I Await a Love That's True

In our village, Vesna, there lived a guy called Vaska Metus, and he had a wife.

"So what?" you'll say. "A lot of people live in this village, and almost all of them have got wives."

But he really hated his wife and would have liked to get rid of her.

"So what!" you'll say again. "A lot of people really hate their wives and would like to get rid of them."

But look. Listen to this. There are lots and lots of people like that, but Metus upped and brought home a second wife while his first was still alive and kicking.

He brought her in and left her in the hallway. And he himself went right inside the hut.

Sitting there at home were his, so to speak, actual wife Galka and Metus's old mother Makarina Savelevna, who considered her son a fool, despite the fact that he provided her with food and drink, and clothed her in print frocks.

The women were cracking sunflower seeds.

There was music and singing on the radio. The wall clock was ticking. The pussy cat was purring, and his relatives pounced on Vaska, telling him he was a drunk.

"Where you been loafing about, yer bastard?!"

"Where?" said Metus, repeating the question, and told them where.

The women started running round the kitchen, thinking that Vaska was now going to set about them.

But he didn't start hitting them, on the contrary, he sat down at the kitchen table, covered with oilcloth, and said in faltering tones: G-glina! I've got to discuss a very important question with you."

"Question, question! What question! What you on about? You'd better lie down, Vasenka, and we'll have a talk tomorrow," replied Galina, in a voice full of tears, and evidently braced for one of Vaska's beatings.

"Sit down, sit down, woman!" repeated Vasily sternly and imperiously, and he began to sing:

"*I await a love that's true,*
*One that's great, that's huge!*

Understand?"

"No, I don't understand," answered Vaska's wife Galina, who sold groceries at a stall at the Livestock Processing Plant.

"Well you soon will. I'll explain everything to you," promised Vasily.

And he explained to Galina that she could pack her bags and clear off back home or wherever else she wanted, seeing as not only did he not love her, not only did he not see in her his ideal, or for that matter any ideal at all, but that he even had a new claimant to her position.

"So that's all there is to it. Great. Easy come, easy go."

Vaska came out with this proverb of unknown origin and thought that that was, as they say, the end of the affair.

But oh no it wasn't.

"Oy-yoy-yoy! Oy, I wish I'd never been born!" howled Galina. "You . . . you . . . you and me are husband and wife! Vasenka!"

Shouting. Crying.

"You and me were never husband and wife. You're telling lies. We shacked up together, that's what happened, we shacked up together, and now I'm giving you a divorce," said Vasily, explaining the formal aspect of the question.

He went on explaining and explaining, meanwhile opening the door into the little hallway, where his newly intended had secreted herself, and shouting: Come on. Come in 'ere!"

His newly intended turned out to be not bad at all, and in the darkness of the hallway even looked something of a beauty. Seeing this, Galina started howling even louder, and the hallway beauty entered the house.

She looked daggers at Galina, and then looked into the corner where the icon was hanging, and then plonked herself down at Makarina Savelevna's feet.

"Forgive me, Mama! Forgive us! You too, Vasily, get down, get down!" she said, sobbing and beating her breast.

They all wept and cried. Even Metus let slip a tear. But, truth to tell, he didn't get down on his knees. He embraced his old ex-"shacked-up" wife, gave her a farewell kiss, and started to push her out the door.

They all wept and cried, only his old mother maintained complete calm.

"You're a fool," she said to her son.

"Why?" said the latter, taking offence.

"A fool. A fool. Down, Vasya. Down!" said his new wife in agreement, beating her head on the floor.

And that's how they started their new life. They lived very well. It was only on the first night that the vexations, as described above, which accompanied the changeovers and re-arrangements, manifested themselves. Afterwards, everything sorted itself out: Galina went off back home to the other end of the village, where her parents lived. She went off, and soon afterwards, according to rumours, she got married to a soldier from a military construction battalion who was billeted in their hut. The soldier had promised to marry her as soon as his term of active service was completed. Whenever she met Metus she pointedly refused to look at him.

The new young Metus couple got off to a surprisingly good and harmonious start, despite the fact that Valya, as the newly intended was called, was a bit pockmarked. She had had smallpox as a child, and the smallpox had left pock marks on her face.

"Smallpox is no big deal," Vasily would tell his mother heatedly, excitedly. "Plenty of people look as if someone's been digging holes in their mug."

And Makarina Savelevna's reasoned response to this was always: "You're a fool and always will be."

"Just you see what a hard worker she is," boasted Vaska.

And his wife Valya really did turn out to be hard working. She got a sucking-pig and a heifer and she fed them very well on slops and leftovers which she brought from the canteen. She worked in the canteen. She did the washing up there.

She fed them, watered them, cared for them, and the sucking pig and the heifer grew as if they'd been reared on vitamins.

She even found time to look after Vaska and Makarina Savelevna too. The long and the short of it was, she took the household into her own hands. Sometimes Vasily didn't even have any idea as to what was going on. What there was in the house, or what there wasn't. And neither did Makarina Savelevna. But Valka knew.

They lived very well. It was harmonious, and it was good, and every now and then Vasily would sing that old song of his:

*I await a love that's true,*
*one that's great, that's huge . . .*

"You oughtn't to sing like that, Vasenka, or you'll put the mockers on our happiness," said his wife, flatteringly pressing herself to the mighty chest of her unlawfully wedded husband.

"I'm only singing. Singing, that's all," replied Vasily stubbornly. "I sing because life is varied and it can be anything and everything. You and me could split up ve-ery easily. Like ships at sea."

"Now, now," said his wife in fear.

"Yes. I sing. Anything and everything is possible. I ought to tell you that you're not at all my ideal."

And lo and behold – he turned out to be right.

Because one fine day along came a guy into the yard and ordered him to hand over the sucking pig and the heifer, since "Valentina Ivanovna sold them thar animals to me through the solicitor".

And the guy started shoving a piece of paper with a crested stamp on it under all their noses.

"Well take a look at this, will you?" said Metus, making the guy an appropriate gesture, and then he dashed headlong round to where his wife worked at the canteen, and there it came to light that his alleged wife had already given in her notice.

"And we don't know where she's gone," chortled her workmates, bold as brass.

Don't know. And no one knew at first. He had to hand over the heifer and the sucking pig, because there's no arguing with a crested stamp – you could get in real trouble, and the next time the guy came round he brought a policeman with him. There were no flies on this guy, by the way. He had a house – a railwayman's box and he'd decided to set up home there. He told Metus that perhaps he even understood him, but seeing as the money had already been paid, there was nothing he could do to help.

So they had to be handed over. And only afterwards was the swindle discovered, namely that Valka had been in cahoots with the railwayman. It came to light that they had come to an agreement ages ago, and had only been waiting, apparently, for the heifer to grow up a bit. Now they began to live under one roof, in the box, and thus Vasya's love came to an end and was smashed like a glass bauble.

All this drove Metus round the bend and he said to his mama: "There, you see, Mama."

And in reply the old woman said to him only: "It's all because you're a fool."

"I await a love that's true . . ." sang Metus and then started planting potatoes in the field, seeing as it was spring. He planted out ten whole perches of potatoes, and almost a whole sackful in the vegetable garden.

Apart from that, he wanted to take legal proceedings against his ex-wife Valentina Ivanovna, on the grounds that she had stolen all his livestock from him, but she had a change of heart, got scared and agreed to give him one hundred and twenty-five roubles as an out-of-court settlement.

Metus used this sum of money to buy himself a motorbike. The motorbike was very old and all sort of rusty, but it possessed one important feature: the pillion was a smart, black, soft, beautiful, sprung saddle from off of a BMW brought back from the war.

Soon there were passengers too, because Metus got married again. How he got married this time is neither here nor there, and maybe it's not even important. All that can be said is that his last wife was no worse than the first two. She wasn't pock-marked or squint-eyed, but just looked a little bit like a mop.

Well, Metus just carried on living in his own sweet way. Completely devoid of passion he sang his "I await a love that's true".

Well then. August came round, the month when the yellow leaves fall and the air turns blue, when migratory birds start to head for home, when the potatoes are earthed up and you have to give a thought as to how to gather them in and where to get hold of a truck to bring in the crop from the field.

On the truck they got was a soldier from the construction battalion, Rafail by name, a person of Eastern origin.

On one occasion, they, Rafail and Metus, went back to Metus's place and started drinking and talking business.

They drank, and his wife didn't interfere because she wasn't at home, and the old woman kept quiet because she couldn't care less.

They drank and talked business, and then Metus started complaining that his motorbike was all rusty and squeaked a lot.

"And the exhaust pipe's bent," he said, resentfully.

"The rings, the pistons, the battery, they'll all have to be replaced, but then you watch her go!" said Rafail, scything the air with his open hand.

*The truck won't go.*
*The starter's bust,*
*From the cab climbs the driver,*
*All grime and dust,*

sang Metus.

And they had another drink.

"The rings, the pistons, the exhaust – we can get all that," said Rafail.

"Where from?" asked Metus in astonishment. "There ain't anywhere."

"Oh-ho-ho!" said the man of Eastern origin, making a wry face. "There's a countryman of mine in town, and he's got rings and pistons and mistons, and we can clean it and sheen it – he's got everything."

"You're lucky then," said Metus in admiration. "You people have fellow countrymen everywhere."

And he immediately set to work.

"Mama," he said officiously. "Tell my wife that she's not to upset herself, we're just going into town for some spare parts."

Mama kept quiet.

"It's all for your benefit. One tries, one tries," explained Vasily, pulling the family savings of forty roubles out of the chest of drawers. "We'll be back by tonight."

"We're going in the truck," explained Private Rafail.

And off they went. But they didn't come back by nightfall.

They didn't come back the next morning either.

Then his new slip of a wife said to old Makarina: "Mama, maybe the traffic cops have got them."

"No, daughter, the traffic cops can't get them, because Rafail is in the army. Only the military police can get them, and then if they did, they would let Vaska go, because he's a civilian," answered the wise old woman.

And she added: "They're off on the bottle somewhere, the parasites."

And sure enough, they'd been on the bottle, and a lot more besides. Private Rafail made his way back to them towards evening. Made his way back under his own steam to be precise, not in the truck. He was holding a guitar with a fine red cord in his hands, and he addressed Makarina Savelevna directly, saying: "That's all there is to it, Ma. Don't weep, don't sob, but your son's in prison and they're going to throw the book at him."

And he told a terrible story of how, once again, Metus's "I await a love that's true" had let him down.

. . . Of course they hadn't found any spare parts, because the wife of his fellow countryman, a fat old cow, told them that he'd gone off somewhere.

"Well, where could he have gone to? Why should he go anywhere?" said the friends, dubiously.

"How should I know," said the old cow, and wouldn't let them in the house.

So then they thought they'd wait for him, and went off to the park of culture and rest, where a wind orchestra was playing, where lectures about Mars and astronauts were being given, and also where they sold tumblers of rosé port.

They were in a trellised summer house, overgrown with ivy.

"I await a love that's true," sang Metus promptly and shook Rafail by the shoulder, who opened one eye and mumbled: Ah! Get off, man. Let me have a rest.

And he lay his head on the table.

Then Metus went out on to the nice gravelled path through the park, and started walking along, admiring the culture that surrounded him, and also the rest.

And suddenly – yes, it really was suddenly and not somehow or other – straight out of the blue, he saw the one whom he'd apparently been waiting for all his life.

"I await a love that's true," he sang once more, as he went up to the woman.

"Really?" she enquired hoarsely, sporting a bruise under her eye, beautiful black hair, earrings, and painted lips with a cigarette between them. There was a ladder in her stocking, but she was as utterly fair and graceful as a fallow deer. "Really?" the woman asked again. "You're not taking the piss, are you?"

"Stop bitching, I love you. Ooh, you're so nice," said Metus, putting his arms round her.

"Oh, get on with you!" said the woman, bursting out laughing just as she'd burst out bitching. "I fancy you. I fancy you, but have you got any cash?"

"Yes, I have," said the simple-hearted Metus. "There you are."

And he showed the woman a ten rouble note.

"Oh! There's a good boy!" said the woman, feeling quite herself, and she sang out:

*'Come on, ol' girl,' says he,*
*'Buy a bottle of booze for me,*
*If you don't buy booze for me,*
*I'll find another ol' girl,' says he.*

Hee-hee-hee."

"One that's great, that's huge," sang Metus in response to her.

Then they drank the booze in the same summerhouse overgrown with ivy, where Rafik had by now finished his rest and was chatting with some people, making frenzied gestures with his hands. He congratulated Metus, lasciviously smacked his lips, took a look at the lady and drank to their health.

Then he stayed behind in the summerhouse, while they went swaying off along the nice paths, arms around each other, smoking and, by their appearance, providing amusement for the young people relaxing there.

And time passed. And night fell over the earth, sowing the dark sky with a fine sprinkling of stars, and the moon shone. It shone and shone, and it shone on the ingenuous festival of love being celebrated by Vasily Metus and the black-haired citizen there in the centre of the park, in the bushes, right behind the plaster-cast statue of the hart.

Then, you see, a policeman showed up. Obviously, the park attendant had told him. The policeman disturbed them. He came up and discovered the love birds, pulled Metus off her, set him on his feet, and somewhat equanimously gave him the following advice: Look 'ere mate, you'd better just clear off out of it nice and quiet like."

And to the citizen he said: And if I catch you 'ere again, Tanya, you'll 'ave yer 'ead shaved, yer tart."

"I wasn't doing nothing," whined Tanya.

Now Metus ought to have heeded the voice of an experienced man, gone and found Rafail, and cleared off out of it, cleared off out of it, hell for leather.

But, fool that he was, he upped and started yelling at the policeman, charged at him like a bull, and let him have it in the head with a love-smitten fist.

The policeman blew his whistle, Metus took another swipe. Rafik came over when he heard the whistle and restrained Metus from any further ill-considered acts.

But no matter how he cajoled, no matter how he pleaded with the policeman, no matter how many mountains of Eastern gold currency he promised him, the policeman was immovable, and Metus was taken away.

"He felt very insulted," explained Rafail. "And well, I wonder, wouldn't you, Ma, if someone started punching your head in, while you were carrying out your official duties, and just offering a bit of good advice."

The old woman burst into tears and said: "I always said he was a fool. Do you think they'll stick him in the nuthouse rather than prison?"

"I don't know. I don't know. Better get some rusks baked for him. What else can you do?"

And Rafail went off, adding in anticipation and by way of a joke: "Don't cry, Mama, or I won't send you any dried apricots."

And so he went off somewhere with his guitar. He didn't even say anything about his truck, where they'd put it for him.

Don't cry, he says, but how can you help it? Eh?

And the old woman cried. She cried, but was already getting together the first food parcel: potatoes, gherkins, rusks.

"What do you think, Maria, will they let him have gherkins?" she asked his slip of a wife.

But she was turned to stone. When she heard what had happened, first of all she turned all red, then she turned to stone and turned speechless.

She was speechless for a few days, and then she spat, and with awesome strength set about carting hay and firewood for the house and digging the potatoes.

Then she made a trip into town and got herself taken on by a recruiter to go and work on the island of Shikotan gutting fish. She didn't go to the trial.

"I'm sorry, Mama," she said, bowing to the old woman. "I'll send you a bit whenever I can, but I can't live with Vaska, because he's a parasite."

"He's a fool," said the old woman.

By this time everyone knew all about what had happened. There was a trial. And Vaska got eighteen months. But they promised him that if he behaved himself he could be freed "halfway through" or sent off to "do compulsory community work at a chemicals plant or somewhere".

"Now just you see, there'll be an amnesty of some sort," people said to Makarina Savelevna to comfort her.

So now Vaska is behind barbed wire. His wives are here and there. Rafail was demobbed and went away.

Vaska was given eighteen months, and no one knows what he is going to do when he comes out. He'll probably start by getting shacked up again.

But for the present no one needs him. Is that the way it is apparently? Who needs him? He hasn't got a wife. Rafail has gone away. Is that the way it is apparently?

No, that's not the way it is.

For old Mama Makarina Savelevna is silently and stubbornly waiting for her fool, whom she gave birth to, brought up, bathed in a tub where he said his first "googy-googy" baby words, nursed him, bought him an ABC book and gave him the strap for getting bad marks at school.

She is waiting, hoping for the money to come from the distant island of Shikotan, for the dried apricots and for the Lord God.

She is waiting, living on potatoes, pickled cucumbers, beetroot, cabbage and mushrooms – in a word, on everything that you don't need to pay a penny piece for and which grows free of charge on the landlords' native land.

# The Reservoir

And yet to start with Bublik seemed to us to be a respectable man. He outbid others and paid a good price for a small two-storeyed house and some tilled land which he bought from the grass widow of Vasil-Vasilek, who was in prison for embezzling the nation's wealth, selling on the side iron roofing, Metlakh tiles and central-heating radiators. Whenever he offered us something "out of neighbourliness" though, we just listened politely to him but did not get involved, preferring to take the path of honesty. Because we were all original inhabitants of Siberia. As if I couldn't get hold of some rubbish from Metlakh in my home town off my own bat? That would be a joke, and anyway it would, to a certain extent, run counter to the policy of improving our life and the principles of mastering the outlying regions of our huge homeland. We're not some kind of kulaks, but these days everyone lives like this, and a sight better than those half-wit kulaks of former days, who overdid things when the time wasn't right and pushed themselves up front without taking anybody else with them. For which they were most severely, but justly, punished.

But – Jesus! Jesus! God Almighty! What for? There was just so much work to do! On Saturdays the gas cylinders had to be delivered. Kozorezov was a smart operator here. Thanks very much, he took care of things, detailed a lorry, and a man . . . And if you wanted raspberries, there they were by the bushful, and if if you wanted strawberries, there were beds of them . . . Fine beautiful sight like that went straight to the head, softened the eye and soothed the soul . . . Fine beautiful sight like that went straight to the head . . .

And the main thing was the reservoir. Jesus! The reservoir! This reservoir was constantly being replenished with crystal clear underground waters, but it was a sheer delight for us on those muggy summer nights. A jolly flock of wayward lads frolicked in its loving waters. And our girlfriends and fiancées like Youth itself, the little kittens, lay on the crisp quartz sand. Preparing for exams or merely succumbing to the usual maidenly dreaming – their future working life, the family, marriage, bringing up the children, the proper relationship between the sexes.

And all around were we, the parents. The women knitting something out of mohair, or talking about who was on holiday and where in the south, or who had bought something – some new acquisition for the family. Colonel Zhestakanov and Professor Burvich playing draughts in the rose willow bushes. Mitya the termite arguing with Lysukhin the physicist about the correlation between the number of degrees of Czech beer and its alcohol content. Someone solving a crossword, another questions of production. And me . . . I look back at it all, and on my word of honour, my heart is overjoyed and bursting. The hungry years of the war come to mind when I was recruited for defence duties, and afterwards – standing number 261 in a queue for flour, with my wife, on a stormy black morning in an archway by the Red Front cinema. My foot turned hard as bast, I just couldn't feel it inside my thin felt boot: we massaged it afterwards, smeared it with goose fat. As I remember all this, so, on my word of honour, I would personally strangle with my own hands all these chatterboxes and whingers, stuffing themselves on kebabs and guzzling Pepsi-Cola! I'd have all those skunks standing in my place in that queue in 1947! Then I'd see what sort of tune they'd be singing, the snotty noses!

And as for that pair of young people, the ones that looked like actors, well to start with we even liked them as well, I won't conceal our gullibility, I won't try and justify us . . .

Bublik the director brought them, together with his pretty-looking singer wife. The only good thing about this nasty piece of work was that as a director, when he came, he made our day by arranging for various celebrities to visit Stuffen Nonsense (that was the name of our housing estate). One minute you'd look and see the singer M. walking by, a towel over his arm and roaring "Glory be, glory be", and the next it would be the conjuror T. delighting everyone by making Zhestakanov's pocket watch disappear and turn up in Mitya the termite's shoe, or else there would be our famous portrait artist Spozhnikov sitting up on high and drawing a picture of the reservoir against a background of its surroundings. It was strange that these clever people were unable to detect Bublik's rotten inside before we did, really strange!

Yet at first sight this pair were the most straightforward of long-haired lads. But then again, it's not for nothing that common folk say that a certain kind of straightforwardness is worse than theft, even though modesty makes man beautiful. One of them was on the tall side, a sporty type with blue eyes. The other one was more puny, a bit swarthy, and more lively. Our girls, our fiancées, almost turned somersaults when they saw all the skill those young men displayed at table tennis. And they weren't the type of lads to pass some tasteless remark or make a tasteless gesture to them, challenging them to a game. No! Look, they just carried on hitting the little white ball, modestly and with dignity, the rats. Until it happened.

And when it did happen, then everyone immediately started shouting that we had realized right from the word go. But precisely what we had realized we had no idea, until there ensued a good, old-fashioned bust-up of the worst sort, the consequences of which are indelible, irreversible, sorrowful and shaming, – now the windows and doors of the dachas are being boarded up, small-time purchasers are swarming all over the place, autumn leaves are rustling, fruit trees are being dug up and removed, and there's no cheer on anyone's face, nothing but weary gloominess, disappointment and fear.

Though if you had a bit of nous, you could have guessed right away. After all, they *went around arm in arm*, not to mention the fact that they patently, patently showed no interest in our girls.

And the latter, the delinquents, were happy to snigger. They gave the little one plaits, just like an Uzbek girl. They made him up with brightly coloured lipstick, and then – oh, that seventeen-year-old Nastya Zhestakanov! – then, using a bit of force, they went and put on his chest, which was rather plump and out of proportion to the rest of his build, a loose-fitting spare bra. What a laugh that was!

And at the time we all thought, mistakenly, that it was fun, and we were laughing away, reckoning the somewhat tasteless prank to be a relatively successful joke. We were just having fun and laughing away, until it happened.

Jesus! I'll never forget it as long as I live. So, the distribution of forces was as follows: There was the reservoir. The pair of them were on a raft near the bank, the girls were nearby, we were sitting in the bushes, but the director Bublik with his pretty-looking singer wife was actually nowhere around.

No sooner had the girls fastened their innocent female adornment onto the younger one's chest, than the elder one jumped up, turned pale, his blue eyes darkened, and he gave Nastya a sharp boxer's jab straight in the solar plexus, which caused the child to fall silently onto the sand, without even a yelp.

We all froze, our mouths wide open. Without a second's delay, he shoved off sharply from the bank, and in the twinkling of an eye the couple were out in the middle of the reservoir, where they set about indulging in some foul, filthy language. The tall one ranted and raged, while the small one only snivelled in answer, but also used swearwords. He even stuck his tongue out at the tall one, at which the latter twitched strangely and howled: "Oh, you tart!" and gave the little one a slap. The latter then fell on his knees and started to kiss his comrade's bare dirty feet, which were half-covered by the lapping waves.

Jesus! Jesus! God Almighty! The latter kicked him as hard as he could, and the first young man gave a piercing scream and found himself in the water. However, this upset the equilibrium of the raft, which lurched and threw the second young man in the water too. Without even gurgling, they began to vanish into the deep. Then they came to the surface again, apparently not knowing how to swim, after which, once again without even gurgling, they went right to the bottom.

And a terrible silence descended.

We all stood there thunderstruck. Like a pack of frightened animals our girls all crowded round Nastya, who was now recovering, women and cleaning women woke up, babes in arms started crying and dogs started barking.

Colonel Zhestakanov was the first to come to his senses. With a cry of "I'll rescue those poofters so they'll answer to a court of law!" the excellent swimmer, who had won various championships more than once in his youth, threw himself into the water and disappeared for a long time. When he came up, he lay on his back resting for a long time, and then, wasting no words, dived down again.

However, neither this second, nor the subsequent dives by Colonel Zhestakanov beneath the surface of the reservoir, produced any positive results. The colonel mumbled: "How could it happen", but the fact was they had disappeared.

We hit on the idea of rushing off to see Bublik, the party responsible, so to speak, for the "festivities". But he had vanished together with his pretty-looking singer wife. A pine-scented wind wandered around their empty dacha, ruffling the lace curtains, an upturned cup of coffee lay on the carpet, its contents spilt over a copy of a glossy magazine, clearly not one published in our country, bright orange, orphaned flowers wilted in beautiful ceramic vases, but Bublik and his pretty-looking singer wife were nowhere to be seen.

When we sent a delegation of our people to him to the musical comedy theatre a few days later, the management told us, looking at the floor, that Bublik had resigned from there completely, and cleared off, his whereabouts was unknown. And it was only later that we understood the reason for the embarrassed demeanour of these honest people, when it was finally ascertained that the whereabouts of the director Bublik was the United States of America, whither he had brazenly emigrated together with his pretty-looking singer wife practically in full view of everyone. Which fact isn't after all so surprising, since in the USA it would apparently be easier for them to pursue that debauchery which in our country has such a strict embargo placed on it. It's not surprising.

But there was something else that was surprising. It was surprising that when the police and the frogmen arrived at the reservoir they could not find anyone at all either. We pleaded with the frogmen, and they tried very hard to cover every centimetre of the bottom, but all in vain. The couple had disappeared.

You know, we talked about it afterwards: damn it, if we had had enough money, – they'd had to go to some real expense anyway – we ought to have drained the lake to figure out what had happened and get to the bottom of things, so that the business would not smack of devilry and religious superstition, and so that there would not be weary despondency, disappointment and fear. But the opportunity was missed, and now we are paying severely for our misguided incredulity, carelessness and dizziness.

Because literally the day after everything allegedly settled down again, the housing estate was ringing with the terrible howls of a man being murdered, a man who turned out to be that lover of nighttime bathing, comrade Zhestakanov. The poor man was close to suffocation, his eyes were popping out of his head, and all he could do was point to a trace of moonlight on the water and keep repeating: "It's them! It's them! There! There!"

Fortified with a glass of vodka, he came to his senses, but kept insisting that at twelve o'clock, all by itself, the raft had floated out to the middle of the water and suddenly two sorrowful skeletons embracing each other had appeared on it, softly singing a song: "Don't be sad, you have all your life ahead of you." So there you are!

Although Zhestakanov was soon being treated by the psychiatrist Tsarkov-Kolomensky, this was no help to anyone. Prof. Burvich, comrade Kozorezov, Mitya the termite and his mother-in-law, Eprev the metal-worker and his colleague Shenopin, Angelina Stepanovna, Eduard Ivanovich, Yury Alexandrovich, Emma Nikolaevna, Fetisov, myself, and even the physicist Lysukhin, who, as a man of science was so shaken by the spectacle that he took to drink dangerously, we all saw and heard skeletons.

We tried to scare them away, shouted at them, and fired double-barrelled shot guns at them – but nothing worked. True, the skeletons were not always visible, but the raft really did float around by itself, and howls, singing, laments, hoarsely whispered vows, smacking kisses and entreaties rang out at night *constantly*!

I'm no Zhestakanov, I wasn't even at the front, nor am I a physicist like Lysukhin, I haven't got a higher education, I'm just an ordinary man, I don't even drink an inordinate amount of vodka, and *I personally swear to you that I heard all this with my own ears!* "My darling! My darling!" – and then a rattling noise enough to make your hair stand on end.

When we had tried everything – guns, stones, and even insecticide – then the end came: the end for us, the end for the estate, the end for the reservoir. So the windows and doors of the dachas are being boarded up, small-time purchasers are swarming all over the place, autumn leaves are rustling, the fruit trees are being dug up, and removed, and there's no cheer on anyone's face, nothing but weary gloominess, disappointment and fear.

Well, what would you expect of us? We're not some sort of mystics or priests, but we're not fools either, to go on living in a place putrescent with debauchery, with skeletal lust gleaming in the moonlight, beckoning, drawing, frightening and leading people straight into psychiatric hospitals, depriving women of their courage, men of their reason, and children of a happy childhood and a clear vision of life's and labour's prospects for the good of our huge homeland.

Jesus! Jesus! God Almighty . . .

# The Spiritual Effusions and Unexpected Death of Fetisov

## I

I am myself, as you can imagine, a very unassuming person despite having had too much of a higher education, and if there is anybody around who says that he's more unassuming than me, then let him stand on an equal level with me, there is room for plenty of us.

I have to say that I graduated from university so long ago that I've even forgotten what kind of a student I was. For a long time now I've been working in a factory. It's all right at the factory because I like it a lot there. I work in the factory every day except Saturdays and Sundays and I get paid twice a month: on the thirteenth I get sixty roubles, and on the twenty-fifth – fifty-two roubles.

And I also get a bonus sometimes worth anywhere between twenty and twenty-five per cent of my monthly salary. So for example, just last month I got about twenty-five roubles, but unfortunately I had two days off work for which I am unable to offer a valid explanation to our – no offence intended, let it be said – somewhat insensitive management.

You see, it's all to do with the fact that several times a day the light in my flat goes out, and why this should happen, I just cannot understand.

I don't do anything with the electricity supply that you're not allowed to – God forbid!

I don't do what some people do, jamming all sorts of things in the electric meter, forks, sticks, strips of paper, to stop it turning round, and there is even some special bit of wire you can use to cheat the meter.

But I don't do anything you're not allowed to with the

electricity supply – only boil up a kettle or fry up some fish for myself on the hot-plate – you can do that, can't you? You shouldn't be punished for that, that's something that's just asking to be done, yet hardly a day goes by for me without a p-phut, and the light's gone out, and that's all there is to it, it's enough to drive you round the bend, all gloom and doom.

I usually just sit there quietly and wait until somebody I know or somebody I don't know comes along and mends my fuses, because I'm afraid to touch them myself.

A lot of people say to me: "Why are you afraid of a fuse, Vasily Konstantinych?"

"I'm afraid of it," I reply, "Because I might get an electric shock off it and fall off the stool."

And that's the truth – when the lights go out, you're not going to catch me touching them – no way, never. I'd rather sit in the dark, I'd rather sit by the window, I'd rather look out the window: watch the stars twinkling, people walking by, young couples kissing and cuddling, and you could ask, what do I need the lights for? – sooner or later someone is going to come along and fix them.

So there I sit. Nice and quiet.

So what – I behave quietly at work too.

For example, there's been a Swallow sweet lying on my desk at work for six months now. I myself never eat sweets and other confectionery under any circumstances anywhere, I'm just keeping the Swallow only for guests.

And the guests, or it would be more correct to say "visitors", more often than not are not the sort of people who eat sweets or halva, you're better off serving them crayfish with some beer or vodka.

One has to say that among them you sometimes find such vermin and riffraff that it's even a disgrace to write about them on paper. They ought to be written about on something else, on sand for example, so that the incoming tide might carry what's been written out to sea to be dissolved in the ocean depths, so that there should be nothing left of such people but the smooth surface of the sand.

Of course this doesn't say much for me as a fighter, that I'm ashamed to stigmatize them on paper – after all, these are the very people who come into our factory demanding something, shouting or whispering about something, these are the very people who time and again sow the seeds of discord, squabbling, gossip and rows in our collective which otherwise runs like clockwork.

Now one day I came into work and I wanted to go up to the first floor. We have a beautiful wooden staircase leading up to the first floor.

I wanted to go up, but I heard a heartfelt female voice coming from the first floor whispering shrilly: He's a bastard. He only comes in whenever he feels like it, and he goes off right after lunch."

I was dumbfounded – could she really be referring, I thought, to one of my future friends from high society? If so, the devil alone knew what a turn up for the books this was.

I was dumbfounded, and then the stairs began to creak and squeak, and with a majestic tread some lady descended, exhibiting the extraordinary beauty of her leg and the lace trimming of her panties.

Who was she, this lady? I don't know, I never will know, and I don't want to know. Perhaps she had no need of crayfish and beer, but maybe she needed a Swallow sweet, but could I really give her a Swallow, if she was spreading gossip about, calling someone a bastard and thus destroying the collective?

No, never. Whoever it might be, even the nicest person in the world, I wouldn't give her a "Swallow", and I think that even from your standpoint you'd agree with me, and if you were in my shoes, you would act exactly the same as me, that is, you wouldn't start inviting her into your office, that is, to sit down at your desk, and you wouldn't start offering her confectionery of various types such a Swallow sweet.

## 2

All the foregoing comprises the spiritual effusions of Fetisov, a man who failed to get into high society.

He tells a lot of lies, does Fetisov. He lies all the time. He's always and forever lying about himself, whenever he opens his mouth. Is he a quiet person? Yes, yes. He's quiet now, of course he's quiet now, he's even quieter than a lot of other people, because he's dead. He says, for example, that he, Fetisov, Uncle Vasya, graduated from university, he says, a long time ago. But that's not true. It's a lie. He never graduated from any university, he finished a course at a technical college, a geological-prospecting college. I don't want to go into details, but everything that Fetisov says about higher education is a lie, and everything that I say is true. Believe me . . .

Or all that stuff about the electric lights in Fetisov's flat.

All his neighbours know perfectly well that he uses a special bit of wire to bypass the meter, and that's why his lights keep blowing. His pals at the television factory made him this gadget that saves him thirty kopecks an hour. Perhaps he's forgotten that the wiring over-heated because of this gadget, and he was rushing around afraid to call the fire brigade in case he got fined?

And as regards his absenteeism from work, the Swallow sweets, the beer and vodka, and the crayfish, I'm not going to say a word, because what is there to say on this score when it's all so clear?

I'll just remark once again that the world at large is full of simple, unassuming people. Simple people are complicated, incomprehensible, mysterious and enigmatic.

I'll tell you straight, I'll tell you true – all the achievements of science and technology demonstrate once again that progress concerns only machines and machinery. A human being, however, has remained, my dear chap, just what he was originally. He's neither good nor bad. He's a human being, and that's all there is to it.

Let's take Fetisov, for example. Well, actually, how can we take him now? It's embarrassing even to put it like that, "Let's take Fetisov", when he's dead. He's already been taken by someone else, no doubt. He's in another world now, if there is another world, and no one knows him, no one knows who he is, or what he is now. He's dead.

He, Vasily Konstatinovich Fetisov, died in rather strange circumstances, if you consider that all his life he fought shy of the bosses and did things to thwart them. However, eventually he grew tired of all this and wanted to progress to high society, but he was not admitted owing to a combination of circumstances that were no one's fault, and consequently he died.

He really was an unassuming man, none more so, and he was good and kind, and perhaps even polite to people – depending on who it was.

I myself, for my part, find it very difficult to make head or tail of the situation and often I can't understand what's what.

And being incapable of grasping what happened, incapable of providing a correct literary interpretation of it, of drawing any conclusions, so to speak, I'll just limit myself to sketching out with a few inadequate, clumsy brush strokes the what, where, when and how of it, but as to the why and wherefore of it – that's beyond my comprehension.

And let me tell you once again – truthfully – he was neither good nor bad. He was a human being, and that's all there is to it. He really was unassuming, and really kind, and sometimes polite to people. Depending on who it was.

Now, were Uncle Vasya Fetisov to hear such beautiful words being used about him, he would undoubtedly burst into tears, and would ask me through his tears for three roubles for a bottle, and he would certainly get it, because I, with thoughts of Eternity and Death, would for my part, dissolve in floods of tears and with trembling hands would press a green note into his worker's hands.

Sleep, dear Uncle Vasya. I am going to describe you in detail now, and I'm also going to relate how you died.

Don't be angry with me for addressing you freely and easily in the familiar form towards the end of this authorial intervention of mine and for speaking of you a bit sort of disrespectfully. You will know that, faced with death, we are all equal – that's the first thing, and the second thing is – it's all clear what's happened to you, because you're dead, but what's going to happen to me – that's not clear, because I've still got my life to live.

## 3

Fetisov always had a perfectly reasonable-looking face, but at one time, as far as his clothes were concerned, he used to look like a deserter from every army of the age: calf-skin boots, blue riding breeches with red piping, a grey ragamuffin cap minus its cockade and a green parka out of which poked a hairy chest and the crumpled lapel of a brown jacket – that was him in his entirety.

He was always involved in a good number of absurd, unpleasant and instructive escapades.

But none of them can compare with the escapade which occurred just before his death, the escapade in which Fetisov's yearning for art led him to a sad end, yet just before this, Fetisov was late for the high society which he had long wanted to enter.

That is to say that the society he wished to enter was of course not exactly the very highest, but none the less it was quite high and consisted of respectable people with whom Fetisov had long since dreamed of establishing friendly relations.

So then. By this time, incidentally, Fetisov had received, quite out of the blue, all of a sudden, a fairly large bonus, given his circumstances – one hundred and twenty-eight roubles, and of this sum he had paid two roubles in trade union dues and given one rouble to a collection for the old woman in the planning department to buy her a retirement present.

It was out of the blue, because although Fetisov knew about, and had been counting on, his quarterly bonus, he also knew or had a hunch that he still owed the accounts office something, a hefty sum of some sort, and that they were going to deduct this sum from his bonus, that it was going to wipe it out altogether and that he, Fetisov, wouldn't see any of his bonus at all.

But – it worked out all right. Oh, Fetisov is not the sort of guy to get his fingers burnt!

So he bought himself a Hungarian-made Modex suit, complete with waistcoat, and wearing new boots from Tsebo and new socks and a new shirt, Fetisov set off on a journey into high society, and what was there left of the old Fetisov? Only the green parka and the ragamuffin cap without the cockade, and so there was this completely new man on a journey into high society, clutching to his throat something wrapped in paper – a present, because today it was the birthday of someone in high society.

Images of his imminent future life in high society flashed through Fetisov's chronically inflamed mind.

There he was, sitting at a table, a starched tablecloth, stretching out his fork to get a sprat from the tin, there he was, conversing with Mineev, the deputy manager, about the thawed-out central-heating pipes in their department's residential block, and about relations between the United Arab Republic and the state of Israel.

And there he was standing up, everyone stopped talking and he tapped the carafe with his fork and spoke. There he was . . . There he was travelling on a trolley bus into high society.

And it was time for him to get off, so as to arrive in high society in time, because, for reasons of decorum, he was by now a little late.

Now the door at the front, which by law is the one that passengers alighting should use, out of spite, wouldn't open. A saddened Fetisov tapped politely on the driver's unbreakable glass window, and the driver, who turned out to be a woman, a female driver, responded along the lines that, as she put it, what the hell was it to do with her if the door didn't open automatically when it should because it was busted.

Mumbling "Well, what am I to do then?", or some such silly phrase, Fetisov headed for the rear door, but then the trolley bus, gently, smoothly, and quickly, started off again to continue its journey through the darkening streets, because the driver, and the conductor, and the passengers, who were in a hurry, had had enough of Fetisov – the fuss and bother he'd caused, and his inability to make a swift exit from either of the two doors of the trolley bus.

A furious Fetisov unexpectedly shouted out loud, like a hooligan: "Where do you think you're going? Stop the bus, you bitch!"

Whereupon he found himself at the police station, because the passengers, who were in a hurry, and who didn't need to get off, were terribly upset by his tactless and unrestrained behaviour, and so the bus stopped by the police station, and there two comrade police officers, leaving the urgent business they were engaged on, expeditiously went and took signed statements from the driver and the conductor and charged Fetisov with hooliganism.

Fetisov was not detained at the station for very long, but it was just long enough for Fetisov's late arrival in high society to turn into a non-appearance on the exact day of the high society birthday.

Because Fetisov, in intending to enter high society, had based all his calculations on his immediately drinking vast amounts of vodka and then talking to everybody, telling everybody everything, and explaining things to them, as a result of which they would take a liking to him and receive him into high society as one of their own.

He could still of course, by way of illustration, have entered high society, but there were too many risky scenarios involved now. In the first place, maybe there'd be no vodka left, yet in the second place, there could be some vodka left, but he didn't know how a thoroughly plastered high society would welcome a sober Fetisov, whose energy level was considerably below theirs, all the more so as Fetisov had not been invited especially, but just sort of by the way, casually.

But anyway, he still went as far as their block and saw the windows of the flat – all yellow and cozy, the shadows of the people moving behind the curtains, and he heard music and shouting: "More, more . . . Where's there some more?"

His spirits even rose a little and he felt like calling in, despite the fact that it was well past midnight, but just then a drunken head stuck itself out of a wide window and started puking onto the street below.

A startled Fetisov jumped back and, fascinated, watched as the liquid, regurgitated out of the head, failed to splatter all over the pavement, but stuck wondrously on the wall, and spread out in the shape an aureole.

Then he went straight off home, selling the present on the way, for it was gastronomic, the parcel contained a bottle of

Stolichnaya vodka, a bottle of "Champagne", some "natural Kamchatka mackerel", a box of Alyonka chocolates and a few sweets that were so hard that they made a rattling noise when they banged against each other.

The present was bought by some young people with Beatle haircuts, wearing flared trousers and bondage chains, who wanted to have a drink but who, unfortunately for them, were too late to buy hard liquor from any of the public retail outlets, owing to the late hour.

When he got home, Fetisov didn't even bother to take his boots off, he just lay down on the double bed in which he had slept alone ever since his wife had departed with some scoundrel, and fell asleep.

And this is the dream he had.

Apparently, he, Vasily Fetisov, born 1929, non-Party member, but a daily reader of all the newspapers, became much loved by society. Because he became a great expert on wall art – painting. He became such a friend of the art, such an expert and authority, that the whole of high society listened to his every word on such matters.

And since high society always has connections with some artist or other, on one occasion Fetisov was picked up and taken to see a certain picture by an artist – a friend of high society.

The man came to the exhibition.

The picture was hanging in front of him.

And the man saw the picture, and looked around.

"That is, that is ideological sabotage," he whispered, somewhat distractedly, turning more and more pale.

And then he fell down, and they took him away to somewhere where he passed away without regaining consciouness.

And no one ever found out what was bad and ideologically harmful about the picture. No one found out or could understand why and in what way it was bad. Fetisov carried the secret with him to the grave.

"It's a great pity," many people thought, "that medical science in our country still hasn't reached the stage where Fetisov could have had a heart operation and been brought back to life. Then he could have got up out of his coffin, told us everything that was on his mind and given us advice as to what one still needed to be wary of . . ."

## 4

A sad man, a sad story, a sad dream, and saddest of all – the finale, whose sadness is reflected in the title of the story.

The fact was that Fetisov died that very night. He died after he had uttered the words in the dream "That is, that is . . .", and all the rest was an apparition. The falling, the fuss and the ardent thoughts of many people were the product of his energetic brain in its last throes.

Yes. He died in his own room on the ground floor of his department's residential block, lying down, still wearing his boots, his Hungarian suit, his English socks, and his linen shirt, alone, having failed that day, and consequently for ever, to get into high society.

Peace be to your remains, Fetisov!

O grieving poplars, shed in sequence your down, and then your green leaves, and then your yellow leaves on his poor little grave!

Snows and blizzards – sweep it clean!

Fetisov isn't going to come any more, he's never going to come and ask to borrow money again.

And I say, fighting back my tears: Come here, Uncle Vasya Fetisov. I've got exactly three roubles for you for a bottle.